A Bitter FUMBLE

Euthal Green

ISBN 979-8-88616-466-4 (paperback)
ISBN 979-8-88616-467-1 (digital)

Christian Faith Publishing
832 Park Avenue
Meadville, PA 16335
www.christianfaithpublishing.com

Printed in the United States of America

Overview

A bitter fumble implies someone has made a bad mistake. The fumble begins in the first chapter and rumbles through to the very end of the book. A visitor's disappearance leads to a futile search that is intricately linked to a jogger, who disclaims any knowledge of the incident. He denies ever meeting the visitor. He is poor and Black and has no representation whereas the victim is a tourist with a strong family connection.

External pressure forces a compromised police department to find the victim and a culprit.

The question of the girl's whereabouts can only be answered by following the two fishermen of Potters Cay Dock on their escapade out to sea and back to land. The finding is indeed bizarre.

1

She tipped quietly across the room to retrieve her jacket from the back of the chair where she had thrown it before going to bed. It was 5:00 a.m., and she didn't want to disturb Nanna, who was in the adjoining room catching up on much-needed rest. Not only was the flight from Seattle to Nassau long, it was tedious and cramped up, like being stuck in a tight crate with nowhere to turn. This was one of the miserable inconveniences that came with traveling.

The short stop at Miami International barely allowed them to stretch their weary legs before they were ushered on a connecting flight to resume the final leg of fatigue. She scribbled a short note on the guest notepad on the nightstand to advise her mother that she was going for an early-morning swim, then she grabbed her phone and a bath towel, slipped on her flip-flop, and pressed the door to a gentle click.

Outside was crisp and warm with the welcoming smell of the jasmine flowers floating everywhere, as it did just before dawn and especially on drafty mornings. There was a unique contrast to the cold, damp November of the upper northwest that called for layers of wrapping and thick, heavy clothing that sent people shuttling to the moderate climate of the Bahamas. The environment was different. No thick wooded forest, no mountainous terrain, and no illicit factory-gushing intolerant pollutants. She could taste the purity of the air. It was cool and as easy to breathe as a ventilator. This was the perfect atmosphere for frolic and outdoor adventure. Ariana glanced around, acutely aware of the eerie absence of noise. There was a curious quietness that awakened the senses to the tiniest of movement: the twitching of the leaves from somewhere, the shuffle of her own steps, and the whisper of breathing out there in the distance. This was certainly different. She could hardly remember a time or a place that was so absent of noise. For her entire life, noise had dominated her world. It was present in the shopping malls and crowded cafés, it overwhelmed the school yard and the endless hustle between slow traffic, and it accompanied the locomotives with carriages of raw material to maintain the lifestyle that she was used to. Noise was an existential part of her existence.

The distinction was obvious from the moment their plane dodged below the thin clouds and descended for landing. Her reaction was predictable. It was just like the millions before her who were enchanted for the first time. She had heard the tale about standing knee-deep in water so clear that a speck on the toe could be seen. Her eyes beamed with excitement, and she could hardly wait to prove the insightful phenomena for herself. The expanse of water was sprinkled with patches of brown corals, white sandbanks, and olive-green seagrass. It was just as alluring as she was told. The shoreline was dotted with hundreds of loiterers standing waist-deep in water, beckoning her to join the intrigue.

Ariana had waited too long for the chance to plunge in. She savored every moment and embraced her opportunity.

The gravel path from the man-made peninsula of their villa twisted between buttonwood hedges and sloped gently eastward toward a large parking lot. She could no longer see the outline of the beach that trailed like an extended lace along the bend of the coastline and out of sight.

To enter the confines of the beach, visitors had to pass through the parking lot that was ringed with lamp poles and large croton trees that concealed an assortment of short-circuit cameras. Ariana walked over and read the oversized caution sign that marked the entrance to the parking lot. It reminded tourists and others to secure personal belongings and lock vehicles and disclaimed responsibility for any losses.

By the time she entered the enclosure, the streetlights were already changing to a dull-yellow glow, a sign that the dawn was fast approaching. The ghostlike shadows of the night had shortened, and some had already vanished. Ariana knew she was nearly there from the granular tidbits that seeped into her flip-flop and the fresh breeze that whisked her hair into disarray. In the distance, the calling of the ocean sounded like the deep breathing of a large slumbering creature. There was awe and excitement and a growing curiosity that pushed her forward.

As she crossed the vacant parking lot, the dry sand became boggy, so she flipped off her slippers and continued barefooted. The pebbly sand and smooth gravels slipped under her feet and felt like marbles between her toes. The area was deserted. She had the complete compound all to herself with zero chance of invasion of privacy at this time of morning.

A line of coconut trees and native croton sloped generously from the parking lot to the high watermark of the beach. She could hardly remember ever being so alone and thought of some of the uncommitted mischief that would favor such remote location. She recalled her parents reminiscing about the time when peace and tranquility reigned in Seattle when they were kids, when they were able to rump and ramble without worry, when there was hardly a fear of leaving the house or car unlocked, when the tramp of trains were seldom and few in between. That was a time beyond her knowledge. She relished this moment and could hardly believe she had transcended time to relive their experience.

Near the high watermark, the sand was compact, damp, and invigorating. The sea had ceded its enticement of the previous day with bits of dead seaweed, a few drifts, and a solid outline of the extent of its boundary. In the early morning mist, the water stretched out dark and mysterious like a huge unexplored plain. She looked on with the eyes of a roving cowboy with an extensive landscape to conquer.

The lull of the wind and the hiss of the waves were reminiscent of something embedded deep in her mind and almost forgotten. It was a class hike through Ape Cave, high up in Mount Rainer. The cave was dark and creepy and stank of decaying moss and mildew. An uncanny echoed followed and repeated their steps for every inch of the way. The passage was narrow and spooky, allowing a person at a time to squeeze through a small slit in the rock.

For a moment her hair bristled and her skin tightened with goose bumps as she memorized the similarities between the threatening darkness and the ominous cave. The obscene hissing and obscured breathing were nerve-racking. None of her classmates wanted to be at the front or the rear of the line. They all wanted to cram through the narrow slit at the same time. The objective was plain and simple: avoid an inconsequential encounter with the monster and get out alive.

She stood at the water's edge and gazed across the dismal plain of bumpy waves, and her bravery slipped away with each breaker that popped up and charged in and held her attention. They purred like cats pestered and restrained, grabbing at the sand and rushing back to sea. She pictured herself surviving that fate in the hideous mountain cave.

In the dull morning haze, a transient steamer ploughed into view, kicking foam at her bow and disrupting the haunting cave experience. The strong wake water tumbled in and broke on the shore, covering her feet with a frothy layer of foam. It fizzed playfully about her ankles, then ran innocently away.

Directly in front of her but across the brooding waves, the thousand-foot-long Paradise Island Bridge that connect the mainland rose high from the water like a monstrous Ferris wheel with a thousand bright lights, curving and descending to the other side at a distance away. The foreboding passage under the bridge was reminiscent of a dark waterbed with two small caution lights warning of possible consequences to those who ventured there. Occasionally, the bridge came alive with the wink of traffic light that suggested that someone was off to an early morning start, but Paradise Island remained huddled in her slumber.

Ariana's took a deep breath and, with resolve, focused on her early mission and took a step into the water. It was cool and soothing, and her fears dissipated, and she had to resist the urge to dive right in. She entered tentatively with a promised to absolutely not risk further than knee deep in the water. This meant that she didn't need to undress; she could hold her dress at a modest height and wade comfortably through. After all, there was no one to notice her indiscretions, and furthermore, she was on vacation and wanted to let off personal flares especially in the absence of her parents.

With the uttermost care, she had placed her phone with her slippers in the fold of her bath towel and left them at a safe distance from the water. And with the carefree disposition of a child, she splashed about and collected pebbles between her toes. The mental tension disappeared, and soon she was rolling in the whip of each wave that lashed her legs and ran away, leaving her standing on dry ground. With greater confidence, she drifted out a little more and became one with the sea. She was amazed at her ability to measure and time the incoming swells and avoid being swamped by jumping waves and defying the rip current that ran parallel to the shore.

A speeding boat whizzed past, followed closely by another and another, sending a succession of swells barreling to the shore. Ariana braced and timed her jump. It was good, nice and high, but she landed on a mound of gravels that slid loosely under her feet and sent her staggering for balance. Another swell surged in and yanked her of her feet and retreated before she could steady herself. She floundered in the strong suck-and-draw current and groped with her toes on the loose pebbles to find firm footing. She twisted and turned with the waves and became buoyant. Her small feet stabbed unsteadily as the bottom shifted and moved beneath her. She tripped and fell headlong into the swash. She dropped her dress and for a moment stood on solid sounding. Her footing was restored, and her confidence returned, and she impulsively grabbed the soaked dress and held it high above her knees and waded for the shore.

That was a close call. She blew a whistle. *I'd better get out of here before I have an accident*, she thought. She didn't expect the heavy turbulence and strong wake water. She didn't know the harbor was sometimes as busy as an interstate highway.

The sand was unstable, and the undertow pulled at her dress and made it heavy and cumbersome. A short wave rushed in unexpectedly and swept her off her feet and sucked her in the middle of the rip. She struggled and kicked furtively, but the beaten sand ridge slipped under her and dropped steeply into deep water.

For a dreadful minute, she was dragged underwater. She screamed as her ragged head popped up, and she panted for air. She tried to scream again, but a choking surge filled her mouth and blocked the sound in her throat. Another cruel wave followed and held her under until she had drunk her fill. Her eyes stared blankly, wide and troubling and burned like she had doused them with methylated spirit. Her chest expanded to bursting point as her frizzled head rose again and sucked in a draught of precious fresh air. She paddled franticly against the waves with her dress opened like a sail steering her away from the land. The fight took its toll, and paranoia set in. The pump in her legs weakened and slowed. Her arms ached and waned so feebly that she could no longer tread water and keep herself from sinking. Her silent tears flowed unabatedly but were diluted and lost in the tide.

"Oh God, don't let me die," she prayed in her heart as her mouth filled with water and her listless head bobbed between the breakers with stringy strands of hair, shielding her eyes and hiding her face. "I don't want to die, I'm only seventeen." Her life flashed into view. She was a mere teenager. Where were all her friends? No more party, no more carousing and hiking, no picnic or going to college. What about her boyfriend. Yes, John. What would he do? "Lord, help me!" she whimpered. "This was the most tragic of all. Another girl will be with him." There were too much to live for. She had to live. She struggled to keep her head above water and breathe, but her beautiful dress was a millstone around her feet, dragging her down. It twirled her like a top in the current, and her head remained buried in the water. Her hands and feet that used to be sturdy and nimble, that were accustomed to swimming in the family pool, were no match for this raging tide. She coughed and spat weakly, but emotion was lost, and no froth ran down the side of her mouth. She found a squeak of energy and struck out with aching limbs. She made no gain; the land continued to back further away.

It was still dark, much too dark for anyone to see the tired arms flailing desperately above the hazy passage. She heard a speed boat spanking heavily in her direction, and she thanked her Maker for sending quick relief. She tried to stay alert and used little snatches of energy to tread water and squeal for help. The speeding boat thumped heavily and passed so close that she tumbled in its wake and dismally sank out of sight. Bubbles clustered around her and gradually brought her bloated body to the surface, where she floated like seaweed in the tide. Her lifeless form shivered feebly as another ringing sound got closer. It was nearby. She sensed that it was near enough to touch. It splashed hideously and steamed away. Was she dreaming, or was it her imagination? She rolled freely in the surf and was sucked downward by the midstream draught. She stayed down. The ringing sound gradually faded like music to a drowsy ear. With her sixth sense, she recognized a shadow moving toward her. Overwhelming joy enraptured her as the dress that was once held modestly above her knees barreled in the current and flared around her slender body. She swirled gently and performed like a ballerina for an unknown audience.

2

The T-shaped peninsula of Porter's Cay lay hooded in the morning haze with a cluster of boats sitting in the harbor like a multitude of game birds on a placid lake. The dawn climbed above the horizon, and gradually, the gray outline of each speck emerged and took on a shape. The dominant streetlights dimmed and faded to irrelevance. And the congested harbor that had always been too small to accommodate the never-ending lull and flow of traffic came to life. There was no space even for a hard-pressed mariner. Many boats were whopped together in twos and threes to command a good location to load or unload cargoes.

Boats of various descriptions were segregated according to their function. Fishing and cargo boats were bunched together on either side of the main thoroughfare that was once the entrance to the old bridge, demanding the attention of all who entered or exited. Mail boats that were the main conduit between the capital and the far-flung islands dominated all three sides of the far eastern end of the cay, leaving no space for anyone outside of their clique. Immediately to the south, separated by an opening not wider than a four-lane highway, was an ultramodern yacht haven flaunting its upscale amenities to the rich and famous.

The western end of the spit was reserved strictly for passenger carriers, fast ferries, and large roll-on-roll-off conveyors. This section was a conglomerate of disorder, and on any given day, it was near impossible to navigate through the thicket of indiscriminately parked vehicles waiting for transport to other destinations.

Potter's Cay has a pulse of its own.

*****

At this time of morning, the dock was quiet and deserted. Revelers and traders had not yet converged to their daily hustle, and only a few people were milling about, determined to beat the sunrise and begin their daily concession. Every night this venue was transformed to an esplanade packed with people from all levels of society and all walks of life. They came in droves to unload, unwind, get intoxicated, get laid, and leave their problems behind.

The litter from overnight peeped from bins and fruit stalls and spilled in the street, giving vivid detail of past indulgencies and waiting to be loaded and trucked away. The sweepers and garbage collectors work diligently to get the place spic and span before daybreak. They were committed to an unchanging system.

Sunrise is the measures of a fisherman's fidelity. It sets the call to duty and issue a verdict on who will be the boss and who will forever be a deckhand. And on this blessed morning, you could count the few people who were up and ready to start the day with a bounce. Occasionally, a drowsy deckhand peeped outside and yawned and stretched and disappeared.

As usual, Timmy was up at the break of day, preparing and organizing for another adventure. He had tried desperately to escape the confines of the dock and his tolerance of a rat race living, but the sea had a hold on him, and like a slave to his habit, he had to return. His boat was his home. He was familiar with the putrid smell of rotting vegetable and overnight food and the clean whiff of salty air. He was accustomed to the reeking scourge of decaying fish guts and the frequent willful and unprovoked brawls. This was his routine, where the predictability of life was as sure as the ebb and flow of the morning tide.

He stood on his deck and rubbed the cobwebs from his eyes and admired the quiet surrounding that was a remarkable contrast to the ruckus celebration of the last few hours. He affectionately pulled a phrase from his chest of clichés and repeated it aloud, "Another day, another dollar!" He looked toward the open sea with expectation as if focusing on a distant object.

Every morning, with speed and cunning, a school of amberjacks scouted the perimeter of the harbor, grabbing morsels of food they knew would be there, and scattering clusters of pilchards from the safe shadows of boats where they gathered to sniff the remains of fish blood and discarded filtrates. He always wanted to tackle one of those large amberjacks but was never prepared nor alert enough to do so. Jacks move quickly. In a flash, they were in and out. Today Timmy was well prepared. For several days, he had watched the run that rolled in with a ridge of water and had programmed it in his brain. He witnessed the shimmering school of fish zip past his boat on their rendezvous, scoring the area, then retreating in fixed alignment to the open waters. If today was no different, this was his opportunity. On the deck was a bowl of conch-slop, a 150-pound test reel of nylon line and a sturdy gaff, strong enough to lift a hundred pounds on deck. He was all set. The tide was right, full, and slack, with the current holes that fed water from one side to the other section of the harbor, completely hidden from view.

He was glad to be up and ready, relishing this moment that had eluded him for so long. He expertly unrolled the line and watched the spool bounce about, leaving a neat curl clear and free from tangle. He examined his hook like a seasoned angler and daubed it in the rich conch-slop until it was irresistibly dripping and hidden. "Just the right teaser." He smiled with satisfaction and tossed the baited line from the boat, then adequately assembled another length to assure that whatever took it had enough scope to run and swallow and set firmly. He secured the other end of the line to a cleat at the stern of the boat, then gleefully set to get an eye opener of Bacardi and coffee.

He stepped away and momentarily returned to the deck and sat on an old beach chair that was once white but was now dinged from overuse and lack of care. His concoction was mixed in a twelve-ounce peaches can. He liked being traditional. He took a sip and placed the can on the deck within arm's reach. It was good, the perfect drink for the night after. He reached and cradled the can gingerly in his hand

and took a deep draft and rested it carefully on the deck and waited. His hands must be free.

He licked his lips and smiled contentedly at the mixture that had become his specialty. He remembered the first time he tasted it. He was working at a warehouse on Blue Hill Road. It was a biting cold December morning. It was so cold that his lips were cracked and dry and turning white. He was forced to warm his crimpled fingers by hiding them deep in his armpit. He observed that one of his colleagues, Victoria, a petite humpback woman, wheeled back and forth with the agility of an athlete bursting with energy and impervious to the cold. She wore no overcoat, and she sipped contentedly on a lone cup of coffee. Eventually, Timmy marshaled the courage to beg her for a drink.

"Hey, Vicky, man I need to beg you for a toke of your coffee. I'm so cold, my bones hurt."

Vicky smiled but didn't make an offer. She simply responded, "Gee, Timmy, I don't think you could drink this stuff," and went about her business.

Timmy pressed, "Come on, Vicky, just a lil' bit, please."

Vicky turned and smiled sheepishly, "Look, Timmy, my coffee ain't coffee."

Timmy was puzzled. He didn't know what to say except, "Well, if you could drink it, I don't see why I can't."

Vicky found a Styrofoam cup and poured a jigger.

Timmy sampled the mixture and looked at his counterpart with a questioning smile. The renowned aroma confirmed that it was coffee, but there was something else that gave an additional kick and a warm and tingling sensation.

After a few more sips, Vicky divulged her secret. "It's Bacardi and coffee," she whispered. "The coffee cuts the scent of the rum, so no one knows what you're drinking, but the thrill remains. Remember"—she waved a finger—"no drinking on the job."

Timmy and Vicky became forever best friends.

Timmy reminisced and smiled. "This deserves a toast. I'll raise my can to Vicky!" It gave him an excuse to take another "swag." He reached for his can but recoiled as a sudden jerk pulled the curl of line over the side of the boat. He stumbled from his seat and grabbed the attached end with trembling hands and pulled the loose line back on deck. In disappointment, he returned to his chair.

"What the heck could that be?" he questioned as he had seen no ridge of water and had detected nothing rushing past his boat. *Maybe it was the swinging of the boat in the changing tide*, he thought.

He hoped the fish would run before the usual clutter of pedestrian and traffic. He wanted to catch it, gut it, and place it on display before the irritable crowd descended on the market. He took another sip of his concoction and sucked in the cool morning air and watched the rim of the horizon slowly come into view. The purplish clouds drifted above the sea, turned floral orange, and thinned like paint on an artist canvas as the sun appeared.

Timmy whispered absentmindedly, "Orange sky in the morning, sailors take warning."

Traffic started to flow in and out and parked in any available spot as the port slowly stumbled to life.

There was another tick, so quiet and indistinct that it could have been caused by the shifting motion of the chair or the riding of the boat against the concrete wharf as the tide crested and turn. Timmy waited and watched. There was another tick, and before he could reach it, the line whisked off the deck and set taut against the waist of the boat.

He jumped from his chair, kicking his precious brew to the side. The can rolled willingly with the inclination of the boat and drained the remainder of its content into the sea. As by consent, the stern of the boat dipped and drifted away from the dock, and the nylon line stretched and strummed like a guitar as it ran toward the southern side of the harbor.

Timmy forgot the peril of a nylon line on an ungloved hand, grabbed the precarious lead, and tried to wrap it around his palm. The line was too taut, and it slipped away, ripping the skin from the index finger of his right hand. Excitement and pain became ally in the quest for the same goal. He hung on. Even though one hand was dripping with blood, he was determined to take the fight to the opponent. He trembled, and his legs shook and became unstable.

There was a nervous excitement, and he had to sit to maintain his composure. There was no doubt about it, the unyielding strength and tenacity definitely belonged to a giant of its kind. Timmy had one desire, and that was to land the monster. He had to win.

He dug in doggedly, relying on his past experience and skill as an angler.

"I'll manipulate it!" He laughed timidly. "I'll play it! Let it run and wear itself out, then wheel it in like a baby. I'm not named Thomas for nothing! I'll land him by the hook or the crook!" he boasted of his cleverness.

He leaned against the rail of the boat for leverage as the bewildered creature scuttled madly against the muddy bottom. The fifty-five-foot boat buoyed like a toy and twisted at right angle and would have turned completely around if her spring lines hadn't prevented further play. A discomfiting feeling crept over Timmy.

"What the frig is this?" he swore at his battered hand. "No jack in the world could pull like this!" He rejected the thought of cutting the line to end the tussle. "No way! I gotta see what this bugger is even if it means being another Hemingway. I'll fight him all day and night if that's what it takes." His mind reflected to the famed story by Ernest Hemingway, where an old man hooked an enormous fish that fought him for days.

As the minutes passed, glee turned to dread, and the ambition of landing a giant amberjack was replaced with the horrid probability of contending with a monstrous sea devil. If captured, the bouncing brute would swish about the deck and create an awful mess. He could imagine the bloody puke and the complete disarray and injury, maybe even death. It was only a few years back that a diver somewhere in the Caribbean was gored to death by one of these creatures that felt threatened. Tim relented.

"Why didn't I think of that?" He slapped his chest. "This is definitely a sea devil."

The fight continued. The brute held its ground, and so did Timmy, and it didn't make its signature jump.

Timmy was so consumed with the struggle that he didn't notice the small gathering at the head of his boat.

"Well, I'll be damned. This is what I call a fight. I wonder what he hooked?" inquired a woman who had thrown her full attention into the skirmish.

"I think he hooked Nassau?" mocked the person next to her.

"Let's put fun an' jokes aside! Be serious now. Did you see how long he was fighting with that thing?" the first woman continued.

"Seriously?" added a third person. "That's a sea devil. I could tell by the way it's running from side to side. Those bitches are strong as ox. You don't sit down an' catch one o' them. Better if he cut the line and let it go."

"Sea devil," interjected another bystander. "If that was a sea devil, that line could never hold it. It would be jumping through the air so much, that line would snap like thread."

Another butted in, "That's gat ta be a bull shark. One o' them big aggressive bitches. If you hook one of them, you could tell your sweet Jesus you' in for a fight—all day an' all night. They don't give in!"

"But do you think a tiger shark could pull that big boat down like that."

The conversation continued with the speaker pointing at the large vessel tilted to one side and swaying out from the dock.

"Maybe it's a great white!" a man teased, trying to gin up fear from the crowd.

"White shark? Now that's silly! Really stupid. This is not Australia. White sharks don't come in this area." This guy was resolute and staunchly defended his statement.

A lady who seemed to have some prominence among the crowd, seized the opportunity to add her prophesy.

"Listen, sonny," she said with a tremor in her voice, "these are the last days. Monsters will rise out of the sea and devour the innocent. With all this wickedness in this town, something gat ta happen. The sign is all over the place. Don't be surprised. I say stay safe, keep yer clothes on, stay out the water, an' pray." Her sermon ended with no conversion.

None on the planet is as inquisitive as the people of Nassau. They streamed in from all over the dock to feast on the bad news and enter their challenges and bets. Passing traffic ground to a halt as nosy drivers slowed to cram on news for the latest gossip. A chorus of horns added to the theater, and the police was called in to disperse an unruly crowd.

By now Timmy was convinced that it was a stubborn sea devil, and it was absolute folly to fight one of them. It was a losing battle. The speckled brute would die before it surrendered. It would run to the perimeter of the harbor, replenish its energy, and begin the tussle all over again. It wasn't worth it. Timmy released the line, and it scraped heavily against the side of the boat and began wear away the tough gel coat in the same way it torn away the skin from his finger. The line made contact with the stiff fiberglass and formed a groove that got warm and blackened. Timmy knew what was about to happen. There was a whisk of smoke, the tension relaxed, the spring lines drooped near the water; and the *Defender* yacht stood upright and drifted to its place at the dock. Timmy was left with mixed feeling. He was relieved that the struggle was over but was disappointed that he did not meet his adversary face-to-face. He looked at the excess line scattered on the deck and tried to picture the enormous devil ray spitting blood as it escaped. After the tremendous letdown, he could not speak to the few bystanders that had waited patiently to see the end of the drama. They broke rank and silently walked away.

Timmy stood pensively on the deck and reflected on the events that had just transpired. Two of his crew knew his disposition and joined him without threading on his thoughts. He looked over the expanse of the harbor, and his eyes zeroed in on a huge gray shadow waddling effortlessly toward them. It passed. The features were unique: submarine shaped, streamline body, sail-like dorsal fin. It glided effortlessly out of sight.

The sun was already streaming through the edge of the heavy drape when Nanna rolled out of bed. Her internal clock seemed to recognize the fact that she was on vacation and withheld its alarm. She pushed the bedroom door open and surveyed the room with the keen interest of a visitor with high expectations. Her eyes fell on the note taped to the entrance lock of the outer door. She paused for a second, then hurried over to investigate. It was unquestionably the familiar scribble of her daughter. She smiled pleasantly at the thought that her daughter had inherited her adventurous spirit. Within the next week, she would explore every nook and cranny and excavated every inch of her new territory. She would be as informed as any of the local inhabitants. There was no need for worry. She placed the note on the bureau and started the percolator and sauntered through her toiletries.

Her motherly instinct besieged her, so she punched her daughter's number for curiosity's sake, and let it ring. There was no answer. She hung up and redialed and let the phone ring for another six times.

Any phone ringing that long, she thought, *would either be answered or intentionally ignored.* She didn't know which was the preferred answer. She hesitated for a moment, then redialed a third time and just let it ring out.

"Anna," she spoke to the device in her hand, "answer the phone!" She was more annoyed than anxious. After a lengthy wait, she slapped the Stop button to quiet the beeping and concluded that her daughter had either rested her phone idly by or was too engaged to answer.

She had all but forgotten the coffeemaker that was singing madly for attention. She poured a cup of black coffee, lit a cigarette, and sat on the couch pulling one leg comfortably under her buttocks while the other fidgeted on the cold marbled floor. She knew that smoking was bad for her health, but habit was the evil that obscured the senses and this one was as much a dependent as vitamins was to the common cold. She was helpless if she didn't have her smoke.

"I'm gonna kick this habit one-a-these day." She blew the smoke casually between her lips and let it curl about her head, knowing she neither possessed the willpower nor the stamina to exert the tiniest effort to defeat her demon. She brushed off the criticisms about the dangers of nicotine and caffeine as sensationalism and unsubstantiated facts created by someone who opposed the sale of these products. As far as she was concerned, coffee and cigarette were the perfect combination to calm the nerves and help with concentration and sleep. She snuffed the exhausted butt in a nearby ashtray and fumbled with the freshly opened pack to start up another.

Nanna had been sitting for less than fifteen minutes but couldn't resist the urge to redial her daughter's number again. Ariana was her only child and her sole companion for these few days. As she had blossomed into a young woman, they had become closer than mother and daughter and were now best friends. This time she let the phone rang and rang until it buzzed angrily and hung up involuntarily. She squeezed the phone and gazed abstractly at the sliding glass door, uncertain of the next course of action. She redialed the zillion times and got only a quick buzzing signal. She took a deep draw on her cigarette, which glowed red and burnt rapidly to a stump. She snuffed it out and lit another.

The coffee went cold and was left untouched. Her focus changed. The desire for breakfast in bed, a morning siesta, and a proposed evening hike at the local Fish Fry fainted from her mind.

"Do not panic," she told herself, "it is still early." But as negative thoughts flooded her mind, she willingly examined them for plausible evidence to embrace.

"Is she lost and can't find her way back?" she questioned and shuffled through several possibilities. "No! She can't be lost. She wouldn't go so far, plus being lost should give her more reasons to call," she reasoned. "Also, being lost doesn't prevent answering your phone."

As more dispiriting thoughts clouded her brain, Nanna felt confused and lonely. She yearned for the reassurance of her husband. "If Amari was here, this would never happen. Ariana would never leave the house without his permission."

Amari was of a Mideastern descent, and although he had mellowed and somewhat assimilated into the Eastern culture, he was a stickler for traditional belief. Women should always be in the protective guidance of men, especially when commuting or going in public settings. Nanna was more liberal and less pressured to follow convention when she was alone with her daughter. Amari was a tower of strength, highly principled, and judicial with his standards. He had sent them on a vacation to Nassau with a plan to joined them within a week, and unless that decision was impossible to keep, it was set in stone.

Nanna resisted the temptation to phone her husband. After all, the matter might be settled quicker than expected.

She fired up the last cigarette from the pack, crumpled the paper, and walked over to sliding door and pulled back the heavy drape and the thin cotton sheer that blocked the exterior light. The only thing that had changed since yesterday was her internal turmoil. The sea was still relatively calm with a steady drone of boats zooming in and rushing out of the harbor. She held her phone like something precious and instinctively glanced at it hoping to see it flickering with a message. That message did not materialize and unwittingly she toyed with the keys and pressed the On button. The phone winked twice and died in her hand. She looked distantly at the blank face, then smiled perceptively. She walked to the door, pulled it ajar, and let in a cool stream of air that diluted the pungent tobacco odor that had settled in the room. She laughed uneasily as a beam of inspiration entered her mind.

"How silly am I?" she croaked. "How come I didn't think of it?" she continued, laughing like she had found something exciting. Her mood changed, and she could hardly restrain her excitement. She glided over to the nightstand and collected her handbag and began rummaging through it. She found it and undid the thin white cord.

"Why didn't I figure it out? Her phone's dead!" She giggled girlishly at her misgivings. "She didn't charge her phone. The dammed phone is dead." She plugged her charger into a nearby socket, and her phone flickered to life.

In fifteen minutes, the phone was live enough, but Nanna realized it was no use trying since neither voice nor text messages would be received by a dead phone. With wrecking nerve, she coaxed herself to stay calm as she waited for another hour to pass. By ten o'clock if she was not back, something had to be done, make an outcry or do something. She had no clue what it would be. Maybe just stand outside and scream. Someone would hear.

Time paced by slowly, and her mind slipped further and further into the gutter. The delay was like painful darts hitting the wrong nerve with painful penetrating pressure. Every shuffle that didn't end up at her door took on a chilling meaning. She was hearing the wrong things, a rasping footstep, turned out to be the riddle of dry leaves scraping the ground. The convincing flutter of fabric was nothing more than the gentle brushing of the curtains against each other. Her senses strained to find a rationale for every sound, and she fixated on things that only a madman would do. She wrung her hand and verbalized her feelings, "That can't be so! No! That can't be so!"

She thumbed through the brochure on the nightstand and unsteadily dialed the numbers for the front desk. The phone answered on the second ring.

"Good afternoon, Atlantis front desk, Mark speaking," the concierge's answered in his usual polite style.

"Good afternoon, sir," Nanna started, trying to steady her voice. "I am a guest at one of your private villas. Me and my daughter checked in yesterday evening." Her voice quavered as she fought back the tears. Her words were muffled, and she paused to catch her breath before continuing, "My daughter went for a walk early this morning and hasn't return. I… I… I don't know what to do." She could not restrain herself any further and broke into a sob.

The concierge was pleasant and very assuring. He relished the moment when he could employ his extensive training and show empathy for his guest.

"I'm sorry, ma'am, did you say this morning?" he responded with concern.

"Yes, about five o'clock this morning," Nanna responded, remembering the time on the note.

"That's about five hours ago. Do you mind me asking her age, ma'am?" he inquired.

"Seventeen!" was the quick reply.

"Well, ma'am, this place is one of the safest places on the island…and there are many places to see. It's still early. Maybe we should give her a little more time. I know how you feel… This has happened a few times before, and on each occasion the individual turned up safely… She'll be back, I can't imagine anything improper happening around here." He paused and waited.

Nanna sniffled emotionally and remained quiet.

The gentleman spoke again. "Did she leave a message to say where she was going?"

"Yes, she did. At the beach," Nanna replied. "I'm scared…is the beach far? She never stayed out long as this… I don't know what to do."

"Well, ma'am," remarked the duty officer, "you're doing the right thing…we'll get her back to you." He consoled Nanna as he wrote down the particulars of the missing girl. "Ma'am," he added, "you can rest at ease. The hotel will leave not a stone unturned to see your daughter's safe return. And for further security, don't hesitate to call the police." He gave Nanna a contact number. "Remember we're in this together. Anything that hurts you or any of our guests hurt us all. You will hear from us soon."

The conversation ended.

*****

Nanna was exhausted but no closer to a solution than when she started. Her head ached, and it felt like an unbearable weight had descended on her shoulders. Her palms became clammy and cold and beads of sweat gathered around her brow. This was the same feeling she had when as a toddler Ariana had slipped from her hand and gone missing in a Target department store. They searched everywhere, and she ran through aisle after aisle, shouting, "Anna! Anna! Anna!" All to no avail. She collapsed, and a store medic was called to revive her. They had just rubbed a dose of smelling salts below her nose when a security guard appeared with the jolly little toddler skipping along with a teddy bear in her arm. He found her in the toy department contentedly talking to the toys and playing by herself.

"No! This can't be happening," Nanna exclaimed. "I must be strong for Ariana." She rushed to the bathroom, twisted the shower nozzle, and doused her head with cold water. It brought temporary relief. She sat upright on the bed and let the cold water drain freely down her shoulders and back. The phone rang. She grabbed it and answered in the middle of the second ring. It was not Ariana. It was Mark, the front desk clerk.

"Hi, ma'am, just checking to remind you to call the police."

She had forgotten. She hung up and dialed police. The answer was prompt and assertive.

"Good evening, Paradise Island Police Station, Constable 974 Sweeting speaking."

The officer sounded bold and confident.

Nanna was more controlled than when she related the matter earlier. "I want to report, sir, my daughter is missing!" She went straight to the point. "I hope you will be able to find her and bring her back."

The officer listened carefully, then spoke.

"How old is your daughter, ma'am?" he asked.

Nanna dutifully answered, "Seventeen, sir."

"Was she alone or with someone?"

"Alone!"

"Did she say where she was going?"

"Yes, she left a note. She was going to the beach."

"Did she say who she was meeting at the beach?"

"She was meeting no one."

"Are you positive?" he asked.

Nanna was somewhat perplexed at this line of question, and her feeling showed in her answer.

"She knows no one here. We are visitors. We just got here last night!"

"Does she have a boyfriend?" the policeman persisted. "Or friends for that matter?"

"Boyfriend?" Nanna was shocked. "We came in from Seattle late yesterday evening, sir. What boyfriend got to do with this?"

"Well, ma'am, the reality is that young people get in contact with each other from anywhere without their parents' knowledge or consent. I'm not saying this is the case, but it happens."

Nanna was not only embarrassed, she was offended by the implications and the officer's brash demeanor. Her voice and attitude changed.

"Sir, my daughter has no contact here! She knows no one here! You are compounding a simple matter."

"I am sorry, madam. I was trying to figure out how a girl would go missing around here." The gruff matter-of-fact attitude was suddenly trying to be humane. "You see, ma'am, this place is festooned with cameras, foot patrols, and security guards. This is one of the safest places on earth. It's not easy for anyone to commit a crime around here unless the victim is an accomplice to it," he boasted.

"So when should I expect to get an answer from you sir?" Nanna asked.

"Well," replied Constable Sweeting with a more understanding attitude, "you must come to the station after forty-eight hours and file a missing person's report. That starts the process." He reverted to his former insensitive, matter-of-fact style of speaking.

Nanna was livid. "Well, what was all that outrageous questioning about?" She hissed between her teeth. "Are you kidding me? Back home you reported an incident when it happens. Any intelligent person knows that time is the enemy of a missing person." She was appalled to be confronted with such ignorant blustering. "Sir," she stated reproachfully, "in two days my child could be dead!"

"Are you a visitor?" the officer asked after a condescending pause.

"Of cause, I am," she blurted out in the most hostile and irritable manner. "As I told you before, we came in yesterday from Seattle, Washington."

"I'm sorry I didn't understand that, ma'am," remarked the distraught policeman.

"Sir, I didn't realize that place of origin was important to solving a problem. I only want to get my daughter back! Whatever it takes to do that, I'm in with it." She was insulted and was at her wits end with this officer who was plainly a pain in the ass.

Nanna was about to hang up. This officer made her feel like a nincompoop. He had implied that her daughter was a promiscuous little brat who was accustomed to having her own way. She halted at the voice on the other end of the line.

"I am very sorry if I offended you, ma'am. It was far from my intention. I honestly would like to know that your daughter is safe and sound, and I promise to do everything in my power to make that happen." He paused for a moment then continued, "We'll need you to come around and file that report. In the meantime, I'll log the matter that you just reported."

She was glad to see an end to the circus and punched the phone in disgust. She was exasperated, confounded, and bitter. She didn't know what the next move should be. She resented the boldness of the policeman and detested his harsh logics. Instead of bringing satisfaction, he had added element of uneasiness to the equation. The conversation left her feeling worse than when she began.

"I'll be dammed if I sit here for two days and wait for someone to show up with my daughter's dead body. That's bullshit! Something must be done!" She was angry, angry at being reduced to an insignificant spectacle in a strange country, angry at the value they put on a matter she deemed to be important. What was the next step? There was no next step. She was as isolated and as alone as a castaway. As much as she hated it, and had restrained herself, the prospective of her daughter's return could not be left to the whims and fancy of people who had nothing at stake. She was out of ideas, and there was only one person she could genuinely turn to.

She paced the room of the prefab cottage that was designed in Germany and shipped to the Bahamas for assembly. The vacationer cared less about this as both the setting and furnishing were designed to enhance the ambience and supply comfortable accommodation. Yesterday the place had surpassed the standard expected; but it had suddenly become poor, distasteful, and almost deplorable. The room had had grown big and empty. The drapes were like heavy decorative canvas that made the place too dark, oppressive, and silent. Her nerve was bothering her, and she cursed her very presence on the island. All the dreadful things that could go wrong seeped into her veins. She stared at the open door and opened a fresh pack of Rothman and fired up another abomination stick. She inhaled deeply and relaxed. The day was gone. She had eaten nothing but wanted nothing. She dialed the number she had attempted all day, and the phone hawked angrily at her. She could take it no longer. She dialed Seattle.

*****

The phone rang a few times that seemed like forever. She was uptight and wanted an immediate answer.

"Answer the phone, Mari! Shit, man! Answer the goddamned phone."

He answered on the third ring, not at all surprised to receive a call from his wife. She had called when they touched down and again when they checked in, bubbling with enthusiasm and dying to begin exploring her new domain.

"Hello," his voice muttered on the other end and waited for her to fill in the blank.

She didn't answer immediately. The pause was unbearable.

"What's the matter, honey? Is anything wrong?" His voice echoed.

She remained quiet contemplating the best way to start.

The line was still open. Amari broke the silence.

"Are you there? Are you all right, Nanna? Can you hear me?"

"I'm here, Mari. I can hear you," she responded in a lackluster manner.

Amari was quick to compare the change from an animated Nanna of yesterday to the presently quiet and subdued person on the line.

"Are you okay? Is anything wrong?" he asked with concerned.

Nanna tried to curb her emotions, but her voice failed as she spoke.

"Anna went out early this morning and hasn't returned."

"Did she say where she was going?" Amari was controlled and unsentimental.

"Yes, swimming."

"Well," Amari responded in the same composed and reserved manner that always made Nanna mad. He was sometimes as stiff as a board. Nothing seemed to pull his trigger. "Anna is a big girl and a strong swimmer. You should cut her a little slack, Nanna. You're on vacation."

"But, Mari, I'm scared," she echoed, "She left since five this morning. It's almost 5:00 p.m. That's a whole day... I'm scared." She hesitated. "I spoke to the police."

"You what? Why did you do that? What did they say?"

"I have to wait for two days," she responded, "then make a formal report. I can't wait." She sobbed. "Am I supposed to sit and wait all that time, suppose something bad happens to her." Amari could sense the terror in his wife's voice, and he knew he needed to say something consoling.

"I'll make a couple o' calls to Nassau and get right back to you," he assured her. "Don't worry, my dear, Anna is a big girl..." He knew he didn't mean it, but it was the reassuring thing to say. "Talk to you soon. All will be well."

She barely whispered an approval.

He hung up.

Nanna was restless but had no alternative but to wait. She was so immersed in her thoughts that when the phone rang, it startled her. She answered cautiously for fear of getting the wrong news. It was Amari on the other end.

"Hello, my dear." Amari paused to be acknowledged before visiting the delicate matter of his daughter's disappearance. "I've spoken to someone. and you should expect a call at any moment," he said.

Her spirit was lifted assuredly. She could always depend on Mari to push the right button. He had formed notable acquaintances in the two years he had spent with a team trying to a procure permits to explore the flats off South Andros and the ridges off Northern Abaco for oil. He had to navigate through a network of technicalities, negotiate special clearances, sponsor too many lunches and offer countless incentive before obtaining the documents. By the end of it, the project was futile, but he had made some invaluable friends. The minister owed him "one," and he had come to collect it.

"Good afternoon, sirrah." Amari identified himself respectfully. Then he added an ice breaker of small talks, then proceeding to the business at hand. "I have a complicated situation that I hope you can help me with," he iterated.

"Yes?" The answer was a question that the other party understood to mean, "Go on, play your card, I'll see if I have a hand that matches."

Amari played his hand. "My wife and daughter went to Nassau yesterday…" He paused to convey the delicacy of the subject.

"Oh great, why didn't you tell me they were coming, I could have made some special arrangements. Remember you scratch my back, I scratch your back." This was a repeat of a well-known chapter.

"My daughter went for a swim this morning and didn't return."

The mood shifted from familiarity to concern. And the minister was quick to empathize.

"This is serious. Did you say she didn't return? Did your wife report it to the police?"

"Yes, she did," Amari wavered, for the first time bending under emotion. He collected himself and continued, "They say she had to wait for two days, then file a missing person's report."

"Two days!" The minister knew the police was within their boundary but wanted to show patronage while hyping up his authority. "Are they out of their cotton-picking mind? That's insanity!" he shot back, taking an offensive stance. "Two days is a frickin' lifetime these days. Don't worry, I'll take care of this right away."

Amari was more than satisfied. He was now reaping the benefits of his labor. This back scratching wasn't so bad after all. It was expedient that he provide details of his wife to his former associate who promised to speed up the process.

"Don't worry about this old buddy, I gat this! I'll light some fire under their feet, an' get the ball rolling right away. I'll give your wife a call an' be on top of everything…like I say, I gat this! Talk to you soon."

Shortly after the conversation ended, Amari phoned his wife to ease her anxieties. He didn't tell her of his inscrutable conversation but told her to expect a phone call from an important person.

Amari reaffirmed his commitment and loyalty to his family and hung up the phone.

In less than an hour after Nanna had spoken to Amari, she received a call from Sergeant Mullings to tell her that he would be over to get a statement about the incident. She guardedly acknowledged the promise while holding on to her first impression. The only reason she had to believe this police officer was different was because the process was initiated by her husband.

"They're all policemen," she chided. "Cut from the same cloth—shallow, arrogant, and full of bullshit. Why should I expect anything different?"

*****

The knock didn't surprise her, and she opened the door without questions. Two plain-clothed men introduced themselves as Sergeant Mullings and Constable Rolle and produced photo identifications as proof. She welcomed them in. After a brief introduction, Mullings went straight to the point.

"Can you give us some detail of your daughter?"

It was easy to repeat the story she had related several times before. This time she was composed and felt confident that the officers were working on her behalf. She was willing to comply with any request to have a good ending to what had started out as a bad ordeal. The cops were eager to show that they understood the seriousness of their mission.

"To begin with, ma'am, we'll need any unwashed item that your daughter had touched or used, like a comb, hairbrush, or pieces of clothing."

Nanna obediently offered a pair of jeans, bra, a comb, and toothbrush. They didn't need all of the items, but Mullings cordially accepted them along with a recent photo and left to commence his investigation.

After the policemen left, Nanna slumped in a chair beaten and hungry. She had been on her feet all day and finally there was a slither of hope. She had eaten nothing since she arrived and suddenly felt as hungry as a wolf. She called for room service.

At daybreak Corporal Been led Rufus, his gray German shepherd by the side door of Nanna's cottage. She was wide awake and elated to see the man who she assumed was a policeman engaged with his dog in what seemed to be a delicate conversation. The man undid his backpack, which perfectly matched his camouflage outfit, and removed a plastic bag with the recognized items. To Been, Rufus was not just a dog; he was a trusted friend and companion. They had worked together for two years and understood the other's mood and temperament. Theirs was a psychological bond. Through dealing with Rufus, Been had developed some instincts of his own. They understood tension and emotion and knew when they had exhausted all possibilities. Rufus adored a mission. It was fun. It was a chance to frisk around outdoors and please his master. With gloved hands, Been opened the plastic pack. The animal's gait was altered. He sat on hunches, with ears pricked, ready to begin. He sniffed each item and grimaced as it was returned to the package.

Rufus led the hunt, straining his collar to the max, insisting that his handler follow and move faster. It was early in the morning, with few occupants on the beach. Rufus paid no attention to the stragglers wandering aimlessly about or the joggers pushing their body to the limit with the hope of getting the physique of someone they saw in a magazine or the undisclosed couple winding down a clandestine mission. The next two hours were crucial; every inch of the compounded had to be examined before it was invaded by sunbathers, loafers, and swimmers. Every degree of the area needed full attention and every questionable article had to be sniffed in rapid succession.

Been shortened Rufus's leash, and he tugged forcefully, all but dragging his master along, sorting and selecting imprints, passing by the coco plum and white button wood trees to the line of croton plants surrounding the parking lot. They crossed the footpath at the entrance to the beach, and the canine stopped abruptly and sniffed the air to reclaim its bearing. Rufus trotted to the beach and paused with one foot raised as if he had suddenly come upon hallowed ground. He eased his leg slowly to the ground and began digging directly in front of him. He uncovered a large beach towel and a pair of red flip-flop that were obviously trampled and accidently buried by the scores of beachgoers. Been collected the items carefully and secured them in a large ziplock bag. Rufus blew the sand from his nose with gratification and continue the hunt.

The next time they stopped was at the water's edge. Rufus sniffed along the high watermark and barked and jumped out of reach of the waves washing across the sand. Eventually, he gave a few deep throated barks, wagged his tail, sat, and looked out to sea. The message was clear: this was where his search ended.

Been understood the conclusion, but to validate his finding, they retraced their steps two more times. On each occasion, they ended in the same spot with the same result.

*****

Mullings and his assistant wasted no time to get started. They huddled in the control room of the hotel, scanning through panels of footages from CCTV cameras that lined the pathways surrounding the villa and leading to the parking lot. This was the fifth time reviewing the information, and for the fifth time, they had come up empty-handed. Each time, the girl was seen ambling casually from her cottage. She crossed the parking lot at the end of the short path that wound to the boundary of the beach. Here the video ended. At precisely 5:29 a.m., a red 1989 Ford Mustang entered the lot from the northeast entrance and parked. A young man in his early thirties in black jogging shorts, black jersey, and white sneakers stepped out. He did a few stretch exercises, bending, twisting, jumping jacks, then began to jog to the south, following the watermark where the sand was firmer.

In a short time the jogger was out of sight. This was a public beach where no cameras were allowed, and except for the lone car, the CCTV showed an empty parking lot. Approximately thirty minutes later, the jogger splashed into view. He made two more laps, then returned to the parking lot. He walked about for about three minutes with his hands clasping the back of his head, then got in his car and drove off.

Unlike the old analogue cameras, everything here was digital. So the operator could randomly select a date and time and view any detail he wanted. In his quest for a connection between the jogger and the missing girl, Mullings combed through footages from previous days and noted that on each occasion, about the same time of day, the same car showed up with the same individual who got out, did the same calisthenics, and left. The inspector and his subordinate were sunk. They spent hours pawing through the machines and found no link whatsoever. This matter was of high priority, and any staff or any shift worker with any related dealings or any activity associated with the beach was drawn into the sphere of investigation.

The day passed with no breakthrough and no lead to follow. News of the case riveted through the government and inadvertently leaked to the press, and the criminal investigating department was ordered to find the girl or find a victim before the international press came flowing in. This was a nightmare of mega-proportion. There was no control to negative publicity. Tourism would fizzle and decline; the economy would suffer tremendously. There was no alternative but to bring this saga to a quick conclusion.

They just couldn't sit and allow this incident to fester and stink like in recent years with the Travolta escapade, then the Nicol debacle. And although there was no famous name attached, there was a kidnapping or perhaps a murder of an American citizen that would automatically get the embassy involved. They could see the headlines blearing out aloud, "UNSAFE COUNTRY! STAY AWAY."

The red phone on desk of the commissioner of police lit up. This was important. Covert operations were never discussed on the phone but emergency was.

This must be an emergency, he thought and wheeled over and decisively lifted the receiver. "Good morning, Benson here," he identified himself even though he was the only person who answered that phone.

"Hey, Benson." The voice was familiar. "This is Nixon," the minister of foreign affairs pined.

The police chief knew exactly what the call was about but decided not to preempt the minister. He hated when politicians put themselves in an investigation.

"Yes, my liege," he answered. Then he asked dutifully, "How can I be of service today?"

He expected a dubious answer but knew there would be some beating around the bush. His job was not sacrosanct. He was a public officer but also a political appointee. He could never be entirely bipartisan if he wanted to keep his job.

"It's about that girl that went missing on Paradise Beach the other day," he implied that it had happened a long time ago. "Do you have anything on that?" His question could be taken as sarcasm, since any positive info would have been filtered to the top.

The top cop remained professional.

"To date, sir, we have no conclusive lead. But I can assure you that our best men are on the case." He didn't want to engage in further discussion but was too dignified to say so. "I'll keep you informed, sir, of any development." He was aware that because of his appointment, the minister was essentially his boss.

The minister made another overture before disconnecting, "Good! We are relying on you." He pressed, "We can't afford negative press." The feeling was mutual, though not shared. "I'll stay in touch."

The call ended.

*****

Mullings studied the report obtained from Corporal Been. He and his dog had found a towel and a pair of slippers that only suggested that the girl was at the beach but did not point to an incident or a lead. In fact, when the report was considered in conjunction with the CCTV recording, the water became muddier than when they began.

Mullings faced the screen, once again frustrated and aghast that he was literally marking time. He zoomed in to the frame where the guy had just stepped out of his car.

"Perhaps he's not as innocent as he looks," he muttered to himself. He snapped a still photo and got a close-up of the car's license plate.

Constable Rolle, his dutiful companion quickly agreed to pursue the link between the jogger and the missing girl.

There was yet another possibility that they had given less thought to. They fast-forwarded to the footage of a white Ford S 10 pickup bearing the name "Paradise Beach Securities" that pulled into the parking lot just before sunrise. In tow was a trolley loaded with beach chairs. Two men exited the truck and unloaded and stacked the chairs piece by piece under the coconut trees that lined the beach. They worked quickly as they knew that as the morning advanced the crowd swarmed and their work would be restricted. When they were through, they reentered their vehicle and left with the trolley in tow. At 9:00 p.m., the beach was officially closed, and that's when they returned and collected all hotel furnishing. Although the beach was not prohibited to them, guests and the public were advised to refrain from swimming at night as lifeguards were no longer on duty. Obviously, these men were company's employees. There was no cause for suspicion, but they might have seen or heard something. They were interviewed.

The interview was a waste of time. They had seen nothing, not even the red Ford Mustang or the jogger or the girl. Mullings returned to his previous hunch.

Within minutes after a request was made to the road traffic department for a cross-checking on a red 1989 Ford Mustang, license plate no. 7389, a matching picture with a home address, age, and the name Calvin Murphy was returned. Randomly selecting an individual from the scene of a crime was no way to score success. But when you have nothing to go on, maybe if you toss mud at the wall, something might stick. It eliminates science and forensics, but if it works, why not use it?

There was certainly nothing to celebrate. They had no cause to link the jogger to the disappearance of the girl. And even if they concluded that he was a suspect, the next question was, What was his motives? People don't kill on instinct. They have reasons. Mullings and Rolle decided to defer scientific deductions in search of a victim. Sometimes a guilty person may be confused with an innocent person because of his quiet demeanor, his command of a good job, and the people he hung out with. This is a headache to investigators. And it took boldness to follow a small lead or investigate what seems insignificant to uncover the truth. Mullings was fearless and ambitious, and he thought that this could be the defining moment of his career. It was indeed a truth-or-consequence game. He needed a perpetrator, and Calvin Murphy was a reasonable choice for a whipping boy.

It took Mullings and Rolle nearly forty-five minutes to navigate the clustered street of downtown Nassau during rush hour to reach their destination at Bahamas Telecoms on John F. Kennedy Drive. They were in pursuit of the strand of hope that led to Calvin Murphy. The idea was to turn another stone that might bring more visibility to their target.

The deputy general manager of accounts greeted the two officers with curiosity.

"Good afternoon, Officers," the deputy introduced himself. "I'm Michael Lambert. How can I help you today?"

"Thank you for accommodating us, sir." Mullings reached forward with outstretched hand. "I'm Sergeant Mullings and"—he pointed to his colleague who extended a hand—"this is Constable Rolle."

"Well, Officers…" Lambert led them past the security officer, who was stationed at a desk overlooking the entrance to the hall, across the highly polished marble floor to a large well-lighted office at the back of the hall. The office provided an excellent view of all who entered or exited the main gate at the back of the building. When they were seated, Lambert directed his remarks to Mullings. "How can I assist, sir?"

"Yes." Mullings fished a black notebook from his breast pocket and opened to a page he had previously marked with an elastic separator. "Yes, sir, do you have a customer by the name of Calvin Murphy?"

Lambert returned an inquiring glance at the two officers. "Are you soliciting information on a customer?"

"Not actually," was the quick reply. "We are doing a preliminary inquiry about this individual, Calvin Murphy. We want to corroborate his residential address at Fork-way Close, Cable Beach."

"Sir, as you may be aware," the accounts manager affirmed, "it is against our policy to share information about our customers."

"We are aware." Mullings was cool and agreeable. "I understand the sensitive nature of these things," he acknowledged. "I also didn't feel like criminalizing the individual by seeking the court assistance in gathering such a small bit of information." Then he lied. "I believed in the presumption of innocence until proven guilty."

"But how do I know you will not be using information I give for malicious purpose?" Lambert opined.

"Sir," Mullings lamented, "I have eighteen years of service, and I'm due for promotion next year. I won't let anything get in the way of that."

Lambert studied Mullings's remark. It was believable. He conceded.

"Gentlemen," responded Lambert hesitantly, "upon your honor, I will accord you this special privilege, which is absolutely confidential."

The two officers showed their photostat and agreed to comply with the manager. Lambert seemed indecisive for a moment, then pivoted in his chair to face his computer.

The two officers left BATELCO with a stated job and its location and banking and phone payment information. The next stop was Commonwealth Bank. They applied for a search warrant just in case this lead took them in a positive direction.

Mullings updated his boss on the direction of the investigation.

5

He picked his way through a network of traffic on Nassau Street negotiating at snail's pace onto Thompson Boulevard. He didn't know what was worst, the heavy traffic or the demented road riddled with holes. At the College of the Bahamas, the traffic came to a virtual standstill. The crossing here was always busy even when it shouldn't be. The students sulked like vagrants crossing the street, daring distraught motorists to run them over. Today was no exception. The narrow-minded, self-conceited, want-to-be-noticed scholars crawled nonchalantly across with the pleasure of a snail that is proud of a new shell. The drivers were left fussing about the degradation of this generation and the dismal hope for the future.

Calvin was familiar with this experience. Over time he developed tolerance and learned to dissent peacefully. Furthermore, the few alternative routes were so ditched with holes and repair work that they offered no escape from the prevailing condition. He slipped a Barry White into his auto-player and sang along. "My first, my last, my everything…" He contented himself that a shortcut through the QE Sports Centre would land him close to his destination, so there was no need to fret about being late. He knew the traffic congestion won't relax until nine thirty when most children were dropped off to school and workers had arrived at their jobs, long after he was at work.

As he hugged the left side of the road and turn onto Independence Highway, the pace picked up, and in minutes, he was gliding around the next roundabout and zooming over Baillou Hill Road. Here the commute favored him as traffic was heavy only in one direction. He took the right turn at the Soldier Road junction and entered the prohibition zone of BEC power plant. This area was off-limits to the public. He paused at the security checkpoint, and although he was a seasoned employee, he complied with the regulations and showed his ID. He was waved through.

The power station was surrounded by a cluster of trees that screened it from the main street. Those who were unaware that something existed behind those trees never bothered to go in that direction. Somehow it managed to bypass the humdrum of the city. The name of Blue Hill Power Station was only mentioned if there was a power outage, after which it returned to obscurity and was hardly ever remembered.

It was 9:20 a.m., ten minutes before the change of the next shift. As was his routine, he parked in his assigned spot, clocked in, and checked his pigeonhole for correspondence and the work schedule for the day. Although he was familiar with it, he reviewed the checklist and time chart for instrument readings, measurements, and gauges and settled to get a peep of the headlines for the day.

The knock at the door hardly distracted him. After all, this was a business place with lots of employees, and at any time, they could expect the odd drop in visitor. Without changing his glance or turning around, he responded, "Come in!"

There was nothing of particular interest in the papers but neither did he think there was a pressing issue from the visitor at this time of morning. The door squeaked open and clicked lightly into place, and he sat stoic and indifferent to the visitor's approach. He was still preoccupied when the new comer initiated a conversation.

"Good morning, sir!" The voice was casual but polite. "I'm here to see Mr. Calvin Meadows."

Calvin looked up. Their uniform clearly said who they were. They were not the typical visitors he expected. His demeanor changed from indifferent to curious, and he stumbled over his words.

"How can I help you… Officers?"

The policemen showed their identifications as one of them, apparently the lead officer, spoke calmly, "We're here to see Mr. Meadows, please."

Calvin dropped the papers on the desk in front of him and swung completely around in his chair and faced the visitors.

"Yes, I am Calvin Meadows," he said, too puzzled to ask for more clarifications before answering. His mind rushed ahead, trying to put into perspective the reason for the visit. He thought of his wife and daughter and the regular commute through an asylum of drivers with multiple personalities. Driving was a nesting ground for accidents. The idea of a police visit on a Monday morning could not be good. He tried to anticipate the nightmare he didn't dream of.

"Is anything wrong officer?" he inquired, somewhat perplexed.

"No! Not at all," was the quick but courteous reply. "We just wonder if you could help us with a few details in a small matter."

The police officer made an effort to unarm his target and lure him into a sense of security.

Calvin breathed freely and offered to help wherever he could. The officers were given priority over a junior employee who came in with a matter that could wait. The BEC worker benevolently offered seats to the policemen, which they politely refused, inferring that their stay would be brief.

"Mr. Meadows," one of the officers said as a matter of introduction, "do you like sports?"

Calvin hesitated. That question caught him off guard. It puzzled him. Why sports? He hesitated for a moment to digest the question. "Dang!" he said under his breath and frowned. He replied, "I guess I do."

"What is your specialty?" the officer pursued.

"I don't have a specialty. I do a little track," Calvin replied.

"And where do you train?" the officer pressed.

"I don't call it training, I call it physical fitness," Calvin explained as he rummaged through his mind to find the connection. *Why would officers come to my job and ask me questions about physical fitness?* he mused. *There must be something behind this.* He knew the rule from his schooldays, which was, answer only what is asked. As a kid, it was his undoing to pour out his heart and get into trouble for saying things and giving information that wasn't requested.

The police jarred him with another question. "Do you jog?"

"Yes, almost every morning." He broke the rule. He was becoming irritated by this physical prying. "Why are you concern about my physical condition?"

The truth was the officers didn't have the slightest interest in his well-being. They were there for one purpose and that didn't include caring about him. The cop smiled thoughtfully and ignored the question and continued.

"And, Mr. Meadows, where do you do your physical training?"

"Do you really want to know?" It was a rhetorical question asked out of annoyance. He pulled himself together and answered, "I don't have favorite places. Sometimes I go to the Western Esplanade, sometimes I go to Goodman's Bay, and occasionally, I go to Paradise Island Beach—all public places."

"Yes, they are public places." The officer did not want to sound offensive. "And it's your prerogative to choose whichever you desire, whenever you desire, we know that," Mullings said sarcastically as if predicting the answer he expected. "And when did you last visit Paradise Island Beach?"

Calvin turns the question over in his mind. He could think of no reason he was asked about his early morning jog. And why Paradise Island? That was ridiculous. He didn't need special permission to go to Paradise Island, people jogged there all the time. All beaches were supposed to be accessible to everyone. That was the law. It sounded like a trap, but he didn't do anything, so he had nothing to fear.

He answered, "I think it was Friday and Saturday."

The sergeant nodded to his associate, who instinctively fished a photo from the folder he carried and handed it to Calvin. "Do you recognize this girl?"

Calvin instantly calculated the significance of the previous questions. They disgusted him. They were trying to connect him to somebody he didn't know. He turned the picture around and studied it.

"I never saw this girl," he said and handed it back. Then he repeated confidently, "I don't recognize her."

The junior officer judiciously took the photograph and quietly examined it as if he were seeing it for the first time. The idea was to apply some measure of psychology and watch for reaction from the subject. Maybe twitching, sweating, being uncomfortable, or even making a statement that wasn't asked for. The tactic was to remain quiet. Who spoke first loses.

Calvin felt like a spectacle on a big stage, crowded by the two men he didn't know. They wanted him to dance to a music that he had never heard and didn't request. He was nervous. Cold sweat trickled down his face and wet his armpit. He could feel the jeering and laughter that comes from the others. He was not prepared for this. He couldn't stay there looking dumb and stupid. He had to say something, but what? The words dropped from his mouth.

"I don't know her."

The senior officer resumed the ritual his subordinate had initiated so well.

"Mr. Meadows," he added, "this young lady went for a swim on Paradise Beach just before sunrise two days ago." He paused and lowered his voice. "She hasn't been seen since."

Everything became clear to Calvin. So that was it. They wanted to tie him to her disappearance.

He hissed out a reply, "I'm sorry about that, but what does that have to do with me? I don't know her! I never met her before."

The officer was not impressed with the answer. He maintained his cool and persisted.

"This is a strange coincidence, Mr. Meadows, shortly after the young lady went for a swim on Saturday morning, you went jogging in the same vicinity. You returned, she didn't. How do you explain that?"

"Explain that?" Calvin was annoyed at the implication, and he didn't hide it. "It must be a coincidence!" Calvin responded in exasperation. "I didn't see anybody when I went jogging. Nobody! That girl or nobody. Are you trying to link me with that lady? This is insane. Was I supposed to be looking for her or something?" Calvin was nearly speechless. "Look, Chief, I hear you. But I don't appreciate your insinuations."

"Sir, it doesn't matter whether you appreciate it or not. We follow the scent wherever it leads," said the senior officer. "We need you to accompany us to CID. We have a few more questions to ask you."

Calvin was furious. "Why am I being arrested? For jogging on a public beach in the morning?"

"No, no, no," the officer was cool and reasonable. "You are not under arrest. We just want to ask you a few questions, and at the same time, you can make a statement about your whereabouts and what you did on that day."

That sounded fair enough. Calvin dispelled his anger.

"There is one thing though. I can't leave the plant unattended. Half of Nassau depends on this plant for power."

The officers understood and assured him that their action was standard. They waited on the outside until a replacement came to relieved Calvin and offered him the privilege to sharing their ride or using his vehicle to go to the CID. Calvin opted to drive.

6

Through the thin sheers, she thought she saw a shadow move passed her living-room window. It pricked her curiosity. She peeped through the slit in the curtain and fell back a few feet.

Outside were three men in camouflaged outfit. Each carried a big gun over his shoulder and wore a black tamp with the letters *RBPF* in white letters at the front of it. A large German shepherd on a leash stood panting as if it was thirsty or exhausted from the morning sun. It was not later than ten o'clock. Much earlier than she had intended to go to the supermarket and before she expected any visitors to come by. She stood still and tried to think up anything that might have brought on this visit. She couldn't. She knew of no infractions with the law.

The three men stood about three paces from her front door and seemed to confer with each other. The man with the dog on the leash left, and the other took their stand by the front door like sentries waiting for their order to arrive. She eased to the front door and peeped through the pinhole, still confounded about the reason for the visit. They gave no indication and, on cue, walked to the door and stopped. She pedaled backward till she reached the enclosure of the kitchen and snatched the phone from the wall and punched her husband's number. It rang once and went to a quick beep. She tried it again.

"Come on, Calvin, pick up. Why did you turn your phone off?" she inquired softly. She wondered, *Why are these people outside?*

She tried the phone again to be certain. She got the same result.

"

"Why are those people out there?" A tingling sensation ran through her fingers, and she squeezed her hands firmly together to get rid of the spasm. "Is something wrong?" she questioned herself. "What's Calvin's been up to?"

The knock on the door was loud. It startled her. She dropped the receiver and let the phone buzz unrestrainedly. She wrung her hands nervously and gathered herself and replaced the phone on the hook. She mustered enough courage to ease closer to get a better look. She knew she had to open but hoped she could delay long enough to get an answer to her most ridiculous question. She also needed advice. She had no experience with dealing with these people. Two of the officers were still glued to the spot in front of the door while their fellow officer and his dog were on a mission, scouting out the premises.

She had to open. She could not continue to pretend that no one was at home. Reluctantly, she unlocked the door.

"Good morning, sirs," she greeted the visitors in her best voice that was heavy with anxiety, weighty enough to sink anything.

"Good morning, ma'am," the courtesy was returned.

"Is there something wrong, sir?" she asked, expecting to get a disappointing answer, although she didn't know why. She knew policemen were typical bearers of bad news. There is never a casual visit. They only visited when something bad happened.

The officers didn't immediately respond, and the wait was nerve-racking.

Eventually, one of them relieved her stress and answered, "Are you Mrs. Meadows?"

"Yeeees." Her answer was stretched with curiosity.

"Is this your residence?"

"Yeees." There was another stress. "And what's this all about?" Her tongue loosened as she regained her feminine composure.

"I have a warrant to search these premises," the policeman said as the man and his dog completed their excursion and joined the company.

"Search these premises?" she questioned in disbelief. "Why? What are you looking for?" Her voice trailed with uneasiness.

The officers discounted her questions and instead handed her a document, which she studied disapprovingly. She didn't know what to look for: the rough indentation of the legal seal; the signature scribbled indistinctly at the bottom, which could have been written by anybody; or the legal jargon explaining the reason for the search. After a few perplexing seconds, the order was returned and the policemen announced their intention to begin.

"May we come in?"

The order was issued like a question, and they pushed by her and entered.

She watched in awe as they ceremoniously fitted their gloves like they were about to working in an infirmary.

The search was demeaning. They assaulted everything, upturning, unstacking, fidgeting, and exposing every aspect of their private life. Nothing was off limit to the rubbery fingers or the scruffy paws and sniffing snout. They tore through the closets and drawers with personal items. They ruffled the sleeping quarters and frisked the grocery cupboard and tumbled amidst the cooking and eating utensils.

At the computer desk, they sieved through papers and collected a dead cell phone and a few flash drives and stowed them safely away. The search produced nothing of significance but left the house in a disheveled mess. They were openly disappointed. They took the computer, two iPads, an external hard drive and left as silently as they came. Nothing was restored.

7

"*I*'m sorry," Mullings said as he saw the suspicious look on Calvin's face. "This is routine. It means nothing." He escorted his bewildered acquaintance passed the main entrance desk down a narrow hallway to a small four-by-six chamber with a wooden bench and a high narrow window.

"Wait here!" he ordered and pushed Calvin in and closed the heavy metal door behind him.

Calvin had parked his car in an accessible spot to conveniently leave when the interview was over. He followed his wardens into the long blue building that looked much like a regular business place with congestion of vehicles wedged into the limited parking spaces. He noticed the crowd of people seated on two long wooden benches at the wall facing a service counter that was framed with thick, clear glass. Several officers manned the counter, and people stood in line to be accessorized for a myriad of reasons. Calvin was not interested in their case but was unfamiliar with the routine and at once joined the line. He was redirected to a window where he emptied his pockets and signed a paper for the items he was leaving. He didn't bother to read fine print; he just signed.

Calvin had few misgivings about anything including being confronted on his job, which had irritated him at first, but then he understood the officers' disposition, and although they were some-what brash, they were just doing their job. He understood. When he was locked in the little cell, he believed them. And when they said it meant nothing, it was just routine, he accepted it. But as the time ticked away and the minutes stretched into hours, he began to look the facts in the face. He didn't need a college education to figure it out. He was betrayed. His confidence fell in his shoes. Their action was contrary to their words. He closed his eyes to reject the notion that he was actually a prisoner. His physical disposition insisted it was true. This confinement was unreal. He was tricked and locked in a small cage with a door reinforced with corrugated steel. How could he be so blind to see? How was he so naïve to believe that there was honor in this ungodly system? He tried to remain calm and examined his options. He needed to make a phone call, to talk to someone, maybe his wife, maybe a lawyer. But from the moment he was left, no one noticed him. He was totally isolated.

The tiny cell opened at an angle that allowed a good view of all who entered and exited the facilities, and he wasn't satisfied that those entering were too absorbed in their own affairs to notice him. It was daunting to think that those he wanted to see didn't come by, but any curious visitor could get whatever details they wanted. Occasionally, an inquiring eye flashed in his direction, and he hid his embarrassment by looking at the floor or counting the tiles as far as his eyes would allow. He preoccupied himself by comparing the number of males to female visitors and tried to endure the long and restless day. He prayed for this torture to come to an end.

It was well past midday when a woman, with whom he had no acquaintance, sauntered up to his cage and impolitely addressed him. For a moment, he became the focus of the entire waiting bench and bystanders.

"Get up punk! You didn't come here to sleep!" she shouted for the world to hear. Then she mocked him with snickering approval, "Next time you're tempted, you'll keep your hands in your pocket or keep clapping."

He was ordered to stick his hands through the grill, and she let the world know he was being cuffed. She fumbled with a bundle of keys and selected the one that unlocked the barricade to his cell and hauled him to an adjacent room to be weighed, measured, finger-printed, and photographed.

"Stand straight!" she ordered. "No slouching!" She slapped the detainee across the stomach and pressed his shoulders hard against the wall as she took his height.

Next, he was aligned to be photographed. The grouch revealed her passion as a tigress.

"What wrong with you? Are you cross-eyed? Look straight at the camera! I'm the tigress you don't mess with, or I'll eat yer lunch."

She took several pictures, growling testily at each exposure.

At fingerprinting, the tigress continued to be ruthless.

"You're holding your fricken hand too stiff. Relax! Relaaax! If these hands were kept in the right place, you wouldn't be here today," she inferred that he was guilty of the crime for which he was accused.

Calvin wondered what she knew.

While being weighed, he was ordered to remove his shoes as it would distort his true weight. He complied. He could never imagine a person being so unpleasant and demeaning and was glad to return to his pothole to avoid the never-ending insults.

For the next four hours, he remained trapped like a bird with a space too small to maneuver. The room was more like a coffin than a holding chamber. The narrow green walls and high ceiling seemed to fold in on him. He felt claustrophobic. There was no furnishing, nothing at all but a wooden bench on the cold tile floor and an ancient washbowl. He stood and waited, but no one showed up to "ask or answer the few questions" for which he was booked. His statement was forgotten. He stood till his leg ached, then he sat on the low bench until the pain in his spine was too intense to hold a decent posture. The people around him became obsolete, and his head became light with fatigue and hunger. He tried to focus on the conspiracy that was building around him, robbing him of his freedom and stripping away his dignity. It was clear that this institution disavowed the presumption of innocence until proven guilty. He couldn't imagine an innocent man being treated the way he was treated. Their justice was just unjust.

He had lost track of how long he was detained and hardly noticed the matron who wheeled a trolley by and callously pushed a paper tray under the space at the bottom of his cell door. He refused to dignify their insults and refused to touch the plate. It stayed where it was placed until the attendant returned and removed it.

As the day wore on, Calvin became bitter, despondent, and depressed. He now understood why policemen were referred to in the most derogatory terms like *pigs, po-po, dick, Babylon,* and even *dogs.* They were insensitive and cruel to even people of good intentions. He had waited all day and was too annoyed to entertain their sarcasm when they strolled by, mask behind impish smiles and false pleasantries. He wished he could strangle both of them in their own spit.

"Look! We're sorry," said Mullings callously. "We had another matter that took longer than we expected." He smiled cunningly.

"What did I do? You locked me up all day! This ain't right." Calvin frisked the air with his hands.

"Hey! Hey, we said we were sorry. Keep your clothes on! You'll be out in a minute." Mulling assumed his pleasant and disarming posture. They really didn't care about his thought. Their main objective was to find a way to conclusively tie him to the missing girl. They didn't tell him of their search. They planned to engineer his performance.

"You're free to go." They opened his cell and cordially dismissed him with a reminder to collect his personal effects at the front desk.

8

The electronics proved to be worthless. The hard drive and flash drive held a ton of unrelated emails, a few Word documents, some spread sheets material, a clutter of song and pictures and a tray-load of stuff from YouTube, TikTok, and Facebook. Literally, there was nothing to advance the case. After a moment of charging, the cell phone beeped to life and the picture of a teenage zoomed in and stayed on the screen. The picture was identical to the one in their possession, so they knew the investigation was on the right track. They had found the culprit. Like a creepy reptile, the crook might have changed his skin and covered his track, but he was still a reptile. They had enough evidence to nail him to the cross.

Mullings flipped through his notebook and found the number for Mrs. Saladou and punched it.

"Good afternoon, ma'am." Mullings was beaming with pride. He identified himself and stated the purpose for the call. "Don't mean to bother you, ma'am, but if it's okay, I'd like to get your input on an item I have in my possession." He wanted to sound less pompous though he couldn't wait for a pat on the back and to be blessed for good police work. "Can you tell me the make and model of your daughter's phone?" He was so accustomed to dealing with vehicles that he spoke about the phone like a vehicle.

Nanna knew exactly what he meant and was happy to supply the information. She remembered the day her husband suggested buying that phone. There was a contention. To her the phone cost too much, but Amari had insisted that a teenager needs a good phone.

"They store more than half of their life on their phone," he argued.

"Yes. It was a Crown Silver Samsung Galaxy S10," she said passionately. "Did you find her?"

"No, ma'am." Mullings didn't want to give out unverified information. "But we are following several leads, and I'm sure we'll wrap up this investigation soon."

Nanna wrung her hand with relief. "Thank you, Officer. Thank you, sir," she exclaimed.

"We'll keep you informed of any developments, ma'am." Mullings politely ended the conversation and hung up.

He paused briefly to make sure the line was clear before he dialed the chief of police. The chief was far above his rung for reporting, but when you're in the clique, there is no barrier to surmount, and you can always jump the line. Mullings's head exploded with anxiety. He knew cell phones were forbidden for sensitive matter, but he was convinced he won't be reprimanded if he spoke to the right person. An ecstatic Mullings dialed the chief of police.

"I have complete confidence in you," the chief said as he absorbed the news with pleasure. Now he had substantive information to pass on up the ladder. "I know I can depend on you," he iterated. "If there is someone who gets result, it's you." He praised his subordinate and dismissed him summarily with the phrase, "Keep me informed of any further progress."

9

Calvin dialed her number for the third time and got no response. He needed someone to talk to. He wanted to discuss the scorching adventure that ate up his day. It was an adventure he had never dreamed of. His head was swollen and jammed with shit. He needed to go to confession, get rid of the shit, dump it on the priest or someone else. Let them deal with it. He pumped the accelerator, oblivious of getting a ticket. Getting home as quick as possible was more important. Luck was not on his side, and he caught every red light for the entire commute. He dodged a few of them and finally crawled into his driveway. Dusk was closing, and the house was dark and quiet. No one was at home. He dialed her phone again and finally got an exchange.

"Calvin, it's so good to hear you. I call you over and over today, and you didn't answer! Seems like your phone was off. I called your work. They say you stepped out, and they'd pass the message. They never called back. I was so worried. Is everything all right?" she spat it all out in one breath.

"Yes, I'm fine, darling. How are you and Sha? Where are you?"

She didn't know of his arrest, and he wasn't going to tell her about it on the phone. He had come home late on several occasions when he had to work overtime, so this time was not a big deal.

"Where are you?" he repeated as he let himself into the house and saw the disarray and confusion.

"Calvin, I am scared. About two thirty today, some police came crawling around the yard. They came with a dog and searched everything. I mean, everywhere! That dog with its dribbly mouth searched through everything, even the dishes and my undies." Her voice trailed with emotion. "After I picked up Sha from school, I was too scared to go back home, so I went to the mall."

"Police! They were at the house? This is interesting! How is Sha?" Sha was their three-year-old daughter. "Where are you now?"

"I'm by my mom's. Sha is fine. She's sleeping. Are you home? I'll be there in a minute."

She threw her few parcels together and was on her way. She was dying to know the rest of the story.

"We'll talk when you reach home." He hung up.

Both Calvin and his wife were intrigued with the other's story. Calvin was especially appalled at the dishonesty of the officers. They knew he would eventually get the full detail of their operation but didn't give a damn about his feeling. They were blatantly mean and discourteous. They had invaded his privacy while pretending to be his friend. It was typical of small-minded individuals to ignore the feeling of others and go after their own impulse. These officers were determined to do whatever it took to satisfy their ambition even if it meant destroying another person in the process. Instead of applying special tactic to their investigation, they chose to look for a shortcut by terrorizing his wife and ransacking his house. This was a bitter pill to swallow and a painful experience to live with.

Calvin walked around his house. Everything was in tack. The street was vacant in all direction with not even a stray dog in sight. The night was cool and intensely quiet with a lone despondent driver peering into the raised hood of his truck at the bend of the road. On a different occasion, Calvin would have graciously offered assistance, but not tonight. The day was long and drawn out, and he was beaten and discouraged.

The road curved like a steep letter *C*, passing his house and straightening out toward Cable Beach. It was not easy to negotiate, and even the best of drivers were forced to slow down, respect the bend or face the consequences. Many of them skidded off the street or collided with the solid concrete wall that set a barrier from going in the sea. This natural outlay made it easy to identify most vehicles as they passed. Calvin watched. No police passed. As he was about to retire, he switched on his exterior lights and pitied the distressed driver who was still standing by his truck in the damp, chilly air.

*****

For the next two days the Murphy family was followed like a shadow and scrutinized thoroughly. They did not see the black Chevrolet Impala creeping behind them, moderating his movement; neither were they aware of the red Toyota Camry that tailgated them and trailed them all over town; and nobody suspected the black Ford S10 pickup that inched its way without problem through traffic, pausing at intervals and monitoring everything they did. At one point Calvin thought it looked like the truck that was broken down for an entire night at the Go-Slow Bend. He pitied the man.

*****

Two days of scrubbing revealed little detail of the suspect. Calvin was born and raised on Abaco Island to a family of modest means. After high school, he attended BTVI, where he studied motor mechanics and joined the Bahamas Electricity Corporation upon completion. He had no prior run in with the law. Sharon, his wife, was born in New Providence, attended the government high school, graduated first in her class, studied accounts at the College of the Bahamas, and now worked at B & B associates as an accountant. This couple was spotless.

Another day passed, and the story of the missing girl controlled the front page of every newspaper in Nassau and Miami, and the foreign press charged in like vultures to clean up what was left. The US consulate quickly pushed a searing ad, blasting the ineffective investigation and warning of a spike in crime. Fear trickled in, and tourists fizzled as expected. People were scared to death to think that that a killer was masquerading among them, and the police was desperate for an arrest. They found the perfect lamb to slaughter.

The next day, bewildered and shaken beyond his imagination, Calvin was accosted and pulled from his job. He had been released and left alone for two days, and just when he thought his worries were behind him, the big bad wolf swooped into town and blew his little house down. They changed the trajectory of the case to change the perception of the people. They picked up a suspect and let everyone know he was assisting them with their investigation.

The greeting was a far contrast to the passive approach of the previous day.

"Mr. Meadows," the two officers said as they dismissed his colleagues and closed on him, "you're under arrest in connection with the disappearance of Ariana Saladou on Saturday, July 12, 1987."

They were totally a different bunch in their attitude and expression.

In shock, he protested and objected to being cuffed.

"What the heck is this again?" he shouted in defiance and faced them and tucked his hands deep in his pocket.

There was a brief scuffle, and Calvin's hands were crudely twisted and then cuffed behind his back. He was forced from his chair and led to the squad car and thrown rudely in the back seat. He bounced on the cushion and the cuffs ratcheted up a bit and bit into the thin flesh around his wrist.

"This cuff's cutting my hand," he complained to the officer planted next to him.

They ignored him and took the shortcut across the QE Sports Center and pulled up at CID headquarters. The braking and twisting on the uneven road were tortuous, and as much as he deplored going along, he was glad when they stopped at the horrid green building.

The station followed the same procedure he'd been through before. They relieved him of all personal items, and they walked down a long corridor and deposited him in a small room at the back of the building. This room was almost a duplicate of his former cell with its green walls, steel door, and extremely high ceiling. There was however a modest upgrade as he now owned a commode, which fell down on sanitary appeal. The small high window was barricaded, but it cast a beam of light on the opposite wall that retreated with the progression of the day.

In this place, protest meant nothing. Either you willingly did as you were told, or you forcibly complied. Calvin understood his predicament as he was hustled from the car and shoved through the rows of curious people and pushed in his cell. The cuffs were removed, and he tried to rub away the ugly scuff marks that stood like a stain and reminded him of the rugged ride and that he was no longer a free man. The system was hard and indifferent. With a whip in one hand and the gavel in the other, the officers were both judge and jury until you were released. This was a fraternity where leaks were not tolerated. What happened there stayed there. Justice was what was expedient and fair play was what brought satisfaction to the troop. When you walked through those doors, you were divested of everything you owned including your rights. You became the property of a hard and indifferent system.

The cage where they put him was called a holding cell, but the only fancy thing about it was its name. And it was just another name for prison. Calvin closed his eyes to unzip and free his mind of horrid stories of brutality and even death that pervaded this place that supposedly came with being an inmate. He had heard the talk that inmates faced one of two choices: confess to a crime they didn't commit or commit to being tortured. The end was sometimes death. He felt a chill creeping over his body like he'd seen a ghost, as the ghostly memory of his uncle drifted in. He had been locked up for being drunk and disorderly. His faults were that he was intoxicated and he used profanity. He was as fit as a fiddle at 9:00 p.m. when he was placed in the cell and dead as a doornail at 6:00 a.m. the next day when it was time for his release. He didn't deserve to die. No one could explain the reasons for the scruff marks on his neck. His neck was broken, and no one knew how, and no one was held responsible, not even his jailer.

Calvin cringed. This was not the place where he wanted to spend the night. He didn't know which imp was waiting in the wing to snuff out his light, so he was wary of everyone. There was a haunting desire to be among trusted people who cared. He wanted to be with his family, with his wife and daughter. He wanted to watch his child grow and be there when she graduated. He wanted to walk her down the aisle. It scared the smut out of him to think that in this place there were victims but no perpetrators. His mother had fainted at his uncle's inquest. He wondered how she would react if she was there when he was carried out in an orange bag.

He sat silently leaning against the wall watching the shaft of light from the tall window shortened and withdrew, leaving the dull illumination of the passage lights. Before now, he didn't notice that there was no light or fixtures in his cell. Night descended on the precinct, quiet and unassuming like a ghost trending toward evil. He wondered if he was the only inmate cramped up in a tiny hole or were there others equally watching and waiting, too scared to breathe. It was odd that the infrequent strutting of the duty officer and the occasional whisper of an unintended visitor brought a degree of comfort and reassurance. He was spooked and stayed awake all night.

Morning came, and he was forgotten.

That's what they do, he thought. *They throw you in a godforsaken place and let you fret over all the terrible things that could be in store for you, then when they do remember that you exist, they take you out and kick your ass.*

Daylight brightened the passageway, and the din of people filled the reception area. The ticking of boots on the tiled floor informed him that someone was headed his way. He stiffened, and his heart beat with the tap of each steps. They stopped by his cell, and he pretended to be distantly asleep. His heart skipped when he noticed that there were three wardens instead of the two he had become accustomed to. The third was a barrel-shaped bouncer with thick arms sticking out from his shoulders like penguin wings. Mullings, in his usual way, demanded that he placed his two hands through the grating.

Calvin was hesitant. "Where am I going now?" he demanded. If he was being released, they won't need handcuffs.

"Look! I ask the question. You answer them," Mullings answered contemptuously. "Don't make this hard on yourself, just put your hand out, dammit!"

Mullings had changed tremendously. He wore a ridge in his forehead and was no longer friendly. He seemed quite irritable.

Calvin complied, and he was shackled and dragged out of his cell and escorted on a long walk like a convict between two officers. They stopped at the extreme back of the complex.

Calvin was not to be taken easily. He was determined to offer resistance in spite of his disadvantage. He pulled and twisted against the strong grip that steered him along.

"Let me go! Where are you taking me? Where are you taking me?" he demanded with eyes fixed on the black satchel carried by the newest member of the team. He knew their answer would perhaps be terrifying, but curiosity forces even the most timid and insecure to peep through creases and pry into the most dangerous and ill-advised things for answer.

The reply was a slap from the newest member of the squad who was itching to establish his hard-knock position.

"Shut up! Shut the fuck up!"

A fist was raised like a hammer ready to bash him to silence.

"I want to know," Calvin persisted. Then he remarked, more in fright than resistance, "I know my rights."

"Chief," the stout policeman injected, "do you want me to silence him?"

"Believe me," Mullings added with a sneer. "He will do a whole lot of talking soon."

There was no question about it; a serious rift had developed between them since their first encounter. Calvin couldn't imagine what had brought about such changes, but his custodian didn't even pretend to be humane. They had rudely snatched him away like someone on their most wanted list and paraded him like a trophy through an inquisitive crowd. They were satisfied to choose him because somebody was too lazy to get of his tail and search for answers. They were blind. Blind as bats. They had come to the table with closed minds. He knew exactly where he would end up if he cooperated. And he knew what would happen if he didn't. Everything was wrong with this fiasco, and he couldn't help being their worst hostage.

The room they entered was painted with the signature lime green with high ceiling and marble-tiled floor. A table big enough to accommodate a feast was stationed in the middle of the room.

His shackles were removed, and he was offered a seat across from his interrogator. He sat with his back to the door. They had it all figured out. Even if escape crossed his mind, it was near impossible to carry out. The position of his seat and the table were instant barriers, and the hall was too long with no exit except the main entrance.

The black satchel was placed in the center of the table and slowly opened. A ziplock bag was selected, and an object wrapped in white hand towel was removed. It was a silver cellular phone. It was handled like something special and place with the greatest of care on the table directly in front of Calvin. Everybody waited and watched. Mullings had saved his best hand and had great expectations. His prisoner didn't budge. He remained silent and confused with an inquiring look on his face.

Mullings was disappointed and furious. His pride was trampled and thrown in his face. He was burned just when the thought he had cornered the culprit. He eyed his suspect maliciously, summing him up as clever and slippery and vowed to squeeze every ounce of truth from him. He was familiar with crooks like this, who thought they were too smooth for themselves. The trick was to make them believe they were winning and that you had lost interest. Time and patience could outfox the fox. Their deception, spying, and trailing had failed miserably. Not one of the private investigators had uncovered an iota of usable information. This guy was proving to be as sharper than they thought.

Mullings looked at his prisoner and smiled artfully. *To beat a criminal, you must think like a criminal. Be cunning, ruthless, and strong.* He picked up the phone and handed it to Calvin. *I will wring every detail out this son o' a bitch if it takes days*, he thought.

"Do you recognize that phone?"

The question was simple, but it was a good way to start.

Start small and grow, be vague, nonspecific. If possible, give the culprit a chance to dig his own grave, he thought.

"No!" was the short pesky answer.

Mullings had his fill of dodging and sidestepping questions. He wanted straight answers, which this style of interrogation didn't allow.

"How did you get this phone?"

They had found the phone in his house and had recovered the prints of two individuals on the phone. One set of prints were Calvin's. This was matching evidence that he had some contact with the missing girl.

"That's not my phone," Calvin answered definitively.

"We believe you, it's not your phone. But we got it from your desk. How did you get it?"

"That's impossible! I'm sure you didn't get that from my desk," he argued.

"Yes! And the time for playing Bo Peep, Mr. Meadows, is gone. You can tell me how you got it."

Mullings was sure he had his man by the breeches and was ready to move in for the kill.

Calvin studied the phone for a while and vaguely remembered the episode while jogging when he ran into a phone ringing on the beach. There was no one else around, so he picked it up and swiped more to see who the caller was then to answer. The screen went black. The phone had used its last reserves of battery. It went dead. Thoughtlessly, he slipped it in his pocket and continued his routine. Later, he absentmindedly took the phone home and placed it on his computer desk and forgot about it.

"I found the phone on the beach," he said in exasperation.

"Now we're getting somewhere. Did you find the owner as well?" The sarcasm was cutting.

"I didn't." He didn't take the bait. He won't let them frustrate him enough to say the wrong thing.

"You didn't what?" The policeman was tacky and edgy. Decorum had left him.

"There was no one else on the beach. I never met the owner."

The dialogue ended for a moment as the officer strutted arrogantly to the other side of the table and picked up the phone. He punched it to life and pushed it in the face of the accused. A display of pictures moved across the screen, paused to be replaced with another picture of the same individual, a girl of about sixteen or seventeen.

Calvin was annoyed and confused. He wanted to say, "Screw yourself and your dammed girl, I don't know her." He might have said it, but he was assailed with another question.

"Phones don't just show up incidentally. They usually have owners. Do you agree, Mr. Meadows?" The implication was clear. "We're more interested in the owner than the phone. Now, where is this girl?" He pointed to the switching pictures on the screen.

"I never met that young lady," Calvin insisted. Then he admitted, "I found the phone. It was ringing. I picked it up. It went dead." He said in frustration, "I should've thrown it back. There was no one on the beach."

"You should have thrown it back," the officer sneered at him.

Calvin understood the eminent threat, and his brain tore through a maze of alternatives and outcomes. It leaped and tumbled in the muddy surf and sunk in the soft white sand that marked the course of his run. Everything ended in insanity. It was just unimaginable what could have happened to this girl on a wide, open beach. They must be looking in the wrong place. He held his head and bawled as he saw himself being cornered because he could not provide a plausible excuse for his action.

"I don't know anything about no girl," he repeated. "I found the phone."

The room fell silent. It was cold and cramped like a packed refrigerator. He shivered with despondency as the individuals before him grew into large hideous monsters. They had weaved their web and twisted their story effectively to look like the truth. It was their weapon.

"We'll need you to tell us what happened to the girl and sign a statement outlining the part you played in her disappearance," said Mullings pointedly.

"Sign a statement! I'm not signing anything! I didn't do anything! I didn't steal, rob, kill, or do anything to anybody!" Calvin was angry and nearly moved to tears.

Mullings paced the floor like he was stalking his assailant, sizing him up for an attack. He stopped abruptly at Calvin's chair. His two stooges stood motionless waiting for instructions.

"Well, well, you are brazen and precise! Very stiff mouthed. We'll see about that!"

The statement was cold and dry, like it was pulled from a corrosive part of hell, and Calvin's gut feeling told him the fight was far from over. He hoped the next round would be on neutral grounds, not isolated in a wing of a building that was as obscured as a dungeon in a medieval castle that few people lived to survive. There was no way to turn for help and useless to scream as screams and struggles were snuffed between the walls. Confrontations always ended the same way.

He placed his hands on the table in front of him to be fettered.

10

The fifty-five-foot *Defender* yacht glided into the harbor with a big load of conchs, buried to her, waist deep in the water. They had been running all night to beat the sunrise and protect their delicate cargo from the rain and harsh sunshine. They maneuvered expertly and moored sternward to the wharf to allow the crew to toss the heavy bunches on either side of the boat. This helped them to establish a temporary territory with their own workspace. The heavy shells fell like concrete blocks and sank to the bottom and settled in heaps on top of each other. The conchs were delighted to be hydrated after eight hours on deck without water. They extended their horns and stretch their fleshly muscles almost entirely out of their shells to get quick refreshment and to try to escape. But they couldn't escape. They were strung together in bunches of five and locked in one spot by the dead weight of other family members.

This was a good trip. The crew was exhausted but elated after four grueling days of bruising work. With satisfaction, they tidied the deck and stored away tools and instruments and turned in for the night. They were in harbor and the danger of losing their cargo was reduced to zero except for two notorious culprits: the human scavenger who scouted around late at night in diving gears to indiscriminately wreaked havoc on unsuspecting fisherman and the never-ending problem of the spotted devil rays that instinctively flowed in at the scent of the catch, to steal an easy share of the slimy delicacy. The weary crew had to be vigilant.

As the haze of early morning melted away, the crew watched in horror as a dozen birdlike shapes hovered menacingly like stealth bombers floating in the shadow of the boat, directly over the stash of conchs. The brutes glided and dived among the razor-sharp shells to get a grip and pull away one bunch of conch after another. The fisherman drove them away by threshing the water franticly with long stick or by spearing them with sharp, unbearded grains. But the devil rays were undeterred. They worked ardently and got their supply and swam a distance away to enjoy it. They drop the load and use their powerful mandibles to crush the shell and feast on the tasty white flesh. Once a conch was taken from the bunch, the creature inexplicably discarded the others and returned for new bunch. This act is repeated until by some means the intruder is stopped or his appetite is appeased. Sea devils can decimate a fisherman's cargo.

"These bitches," Timmy swore aloud and insisted that he would murder a few of them before the day was done. He rushed to the bow of his boat and grabbed an unstrapped harpoon and hurled it with all his strength. "Bastards!" He shouted and missed clean. The animal saw the shadow of the missile and glided out of range, then circled back and tauntingly returned to the goods.

Tim remembered a few days ago he had encountered a monster that stretched his endurance and left him with a scarred finger. That day was different; he was wishing for luck. Today he didn't care about amberjacks or other game fish; they were not his enemy. These bird-beaked creatures were a pest, and if he didn't eliminate them, he would surely watch his hard-earned money evaporate before his eyes. He strapped two hooks to the cable on the electric reel that was still in the boat. He buried one hooks with conch slop and baited the other with a discarded yellow grunt. He slid the bait over the side of the mother ship and jumped into the fifteen-foot whaler that was resting at her side and positioned himself for action.

"I'm gonna catch one of these sons-a-bitches today," he boasted, giving no thoughts to how he would dispose of the creature once it was caught.

He tossed the cable in; and the devil rays, in typical fashion, scattered at the noise and circled the premises to examine the throw.

They didn't take the bait. It was not as tempting as the heap of mollusks lying on the bottom. Timmy wheeled off what he estimated to be an adequate length of cable for a run and a catch and challenged them to think it was all loose food. His mind was made up. "I'm gonna teach one of these bitches a lesson today." He released the extra cable overboard, wrapped the holding end around the cleat at the bow of the whaler, and waited.

The take was quick, too quick to be controlled. It had to be some hungry creature nosing around to snag an easy morsel rather than scrounging for its own food. The cable rang out and stretched taut, and the whaler was caught in a swing between the rigid rope attached to the mother ship and the slim wire cable racing toward the other side of the harbor. Tim tried to pull the cable but got no traction as the smooth metal slipped through his wet fingers. His enthusiasm rose beyond the desire to simply catch a devil ray to the ecstasy of comparing his catch with other anglers. He was sure he had something suitable to win any contest. But he had to land it. Hooking it was just the beginning of the contest. He had to land whatever was on the other end, and he trembled with anxiety. He spoke to the water and anyone who would hear.

"I gat the son-o-a-bitch!" he exclaimed. "If he's bad, let him break this fricken cable."

He expected no one to hear as most people were still huddled in their bunks at this time of morning.

"Bring me a pair of gloves!" he shouted in the direction of his boat. "Somebody bring me a pair of gloves! Hurry, bring me a pair of gloves." He hardly moved his eye off the cable that ran erratically through the water, then rushed in and scrapped madly against the hull and raced uncontrollably from side to sides. The cable remained taut and stationary, just long enough to moan and cut away the sturdy rubber railing of the fiberglass boat.

Someone peeped from the cabin. It was Bengy, a recent hired hand who had enlisted to pay for his indiscretions. Timmy believed that everyone should be given a chance, and when he caught the young man trying to swipe his best fishing rods, he scolded him and offered him the rod and a job. This was his second chance. The event was vivid as daylight. The booming voice at his back and a strong grip pinned him at the shoulder.

"Sonny! Do you like fishing?"

Bengy was so surprised and afraid he nearly peed his pants. He tried to break free, but the other man was stronger. Eventually, his wiggling stopped, and he gave up the fight. Through his fright, he answered, "No! I don't. Now let me go!"

"Perhaps I should call the police," Timmy threatened and that remark quieted the would-be thief.

Bengy detested the word *police*. The jail was like home to him; he had only been free for the past two days.

"Come on, jump on the truck. I'll show you how to use it. I'll let you have it if you promise to pay for it."

And so Bengy was hired.

Bengy later bashfully revealed that he had been to prison twenty-seven times in his young twenty-one years. He had finally found a home and someone who understood and accepted him. He recognized the voice in the dinghy and straddled the side of the ship to assist his mentor.

"Get me a glove!"

Gloves were commonplace on the *Uncloudy Day*, and almost instantly, a pair was tossed into the stricken dinghy. A barefooted Bengy in jeans and T-shirt leaped in after the gloves daring the assailant to beat two warriors. At that very moment, the cable went limp and drooped without a stir. There could only be one reason for this: whatever was fighting so desperately had escaped. There was nothing unusual about this; fish get off all the time. But Timmy's heart fell. This one was different. He was almost breaking with disappointment. He slowly pulled the cable at the bottom of the dinghy, disgusted by the thought that he had almost succeeded. He cussed his bad luck and gazed in the water.

"*Almost* shouldn't be a word," he sulked. "For either you do or you don't. It's an excuse, a leaning pole for ineffectiveness." He was still griping over his loss when a large looming shadow drifted into view. He looked at the shadow in amazement and regret that he had loss the short fight. But all was not bad. The army of stingrays that plagued them had all disappeared.

"They'll be back," Timmy whispered. "And when they do, I'll be ready. I'll give 'em the fight of their life." He left the baited line in the water and tried to undo the cable that had drawn tight around the cleat.

He took his time and fingered the cable, knowing that if left unattended for a while, he would never be able to straighten the kink. He worked diligently at the cable. The stingrays vacated the area, and all was relaxed and quiet. Then it happened. The cable swished madly from the boat, and before he could act, Timmy's hand was clamped firmly between the cable and the fiberglass hull. The steel sizzled through the soft flesh of his palm, sprinkling blood like a pressurized pipe. Timmy fell to his knees and tried daringly to lift the wire from slicing through his entire palm.

"Oh, Jesus!" he winced. "My hand! My hand!" He bit his lip and swallowed all the expletives that bubbled to the surface. "Oh, gawd!" he whispered as the cable fiddled a haunting tune. He couldn't get enough purchase to free his hand.

"Bengy! Oh my gawd, this thing is cutting through my hand! Come quick, catch this cable and pull it! Oh Jesus!" he mumbled and bit his lips.

Bengy rushed forward but stopped abruptly as the little craft dipped dangerously at the bow and threatened to capsize if he makes another step. And the scoundrel on the other end didn't give an inch. Instead, it scurried madly, like it was caught in a trap and went striking at everything to find a way out. Timmy's hand was pinned to the spot, and Bengy was torn to pieces that he could do nothing but watch the foray between the man that he loved and the beast that he feared. Clots of blood formed over Timmy's palm, and the hand expanded like a rubber tube. The blood gathered on the bow and dribbled like an hourglass keeping a gruesome account of a nasty fight.

If his entire hand had been chopped off, the pain could not have been so intense. It was like being skinned alive. A synonymous comparison was being scalped, only this time from the palm. It was the most awful thing that could happen to a man other than the loss of his brain. He gritted his teeth, and like a true soldier, he closed his eyes and wrestled with the pain. He lay on his stomach and bent over until his head touched the water and flailed helplessly to grab the cable that stretched beyond his reach. All he needed was a small opening to squeeze his hand free, but the smooth wire slipped way and gave him nothing.

The creature tumbled and ploughed through the water, and the hook sunk deeper in its gullet and held firmer. It continued the rampage, assaulting anything and everything in its path. It bumped hard into the shallow bottom and set off a mud bath in what was always transparent water. But the resilient cable did its job, holding its part in the battle, and Timmy remained stuck between the wire and the boat.

"Get a knife! Dammit, somebody get a knife, a pliers or something. Dammit!" he swore, which was not his practice. He shouted at the head that appeared at a cabin window. "Don't just stand there like a fricken prick! Get me a knife!" Timmy bellowed as the pain rippled through his arm and cramped his shoulder. He made another futile attempt to wrap the cold steel around the other hand to get leverage to free himself, but with agility gone, he was too slow and clumsy. By now his sixth sense told him that his adversary was definitely not a stingray. Stingrays always leaped out of the water when they were surprised, excited, or cornered. This creature did not leap. It stayed down, rooting at things it couldn't undo.

Bengy balanced gingerly on the waist of the whaler as the rope hitched to the transom and to the mother ship, extended, and tightened. And the skiff with its two occupants and a fifteen-horsepower mercury engine were briefly hoisted out of the water and dropped simultaneously.

A head appeared again, and a young man staggered onto the deck and repeated the captain's order, conveniently adding an extra expletive as he ducked out of sight to fill the order.

"Get a knife! Dammit!" Timmy swore. "Somebody get a knife and hurry!"

At last, a man with a large hunting knife charged forward. He looked at the dinghy dangling insecurely and hesitated.

"Cut the rope, dammit! Cut the fricken rope!"

The whaler dropped in the water like a log and jerked around, throwing the two occupants off their feet. Timmy was free. The hand was liberated, and like a sick child, he looked for comfort and cradled it in his bosom.

The skiff careened to one side and zigzagged unsteadily, straightened out, and narrowly missed the steel hull of a mail boat and turned toward the passage that ran like a road through the middle of the harbor. The skiff dipped and splashed in the headwind and current and darted toward the west.

11

They stopped by his cage. There were three of them and a black satchel. Mullings looked at the man with his back turned to them. He had shown disdain, refused to cooperate, and didn't show a grain of remorse. Getting information from him was like extract a tooth from a timid and insecure patient. He gave them nothing. They ran his profile and found nothing: no political affiliation and no association that might lead to public scrutiny. He was like a Topsy who had dropped from the sky. Perhaps he was one of them who had crept in and got naturalized. He wasn't a grifter; he had a good job and a house. Maybe he had an appetite for young girls too, especially spring breakers, and this was an extension of his habit. There were many questions but limited time to search for answers.

Mullings eyed his prisoner suspiciously and began with what seemed to be a ridiculous statement:

"Tell us the truth, and we'll let you go."

For the nth time Calvin was badgered with the same questions. Obviously, they thought he was a nitwit or his answer meant nothing to them. It simply went through one ear and came out through the other. He was cross and counting his words arrogantly.

"I…don't…know…about no girl."

"Are you being rude, young fellow?" Mullings threatened sarcastically. "I asked you a civil question. Where is the girl?"

"Like I said," Calvin iterated, trying to suppress his anger. His hand was in the lion's mouth; he had to be cautious how he wiggled it out. He had to avoid injuring himself at all cost. Respect was due even if he didn't want to give it. It was amazing how they repeated the same thing but wanted a different result. "I've never met that girl," he said with bitterness in his voice. "Like I told you, I don't know her."

Mullings pressed his face against the steel grating until they were only inches apart. "You dirty little scoundrel," he mouthed with a clinched fist.

Droplet of saliva sprinkled Calvin's face, and he turned to avoid the tiny mist.

The policeman though it was being rude. He could not allow such disrespect from a detainee. Mullings didn't know what he would have done if the door wasn't locked. He lost his cool.

"You couldn't wait to get your grubby paws on that girl. I know fellows like you—hang around the hotels stalking tourist. I bet you licked your chops when you saw that little white girl all alone," he sneered. "I want to know what you did with her when you were through."

"Through?" Calvin bleated in annoyance. "What do you take me for, a psycho? I don't hang out at hotels, and I don't go around looking for anyone. I went jogging. I'm not a criminal! You've got the wrong man arrested!"

"I see," said Mullings cagily and spoke as if to his companions. "We see this attitude all the time. They lie through their teeth." He turned his gaze back to Calvin. "Tell us what else you did while you were jogging."

Calvin shrugged. "Jogging is jogging. You run. That's all you do, nothing else."

Mullings nodded in the direction of his associates who stood by like vultures ready to flock in and devour their prey.

Calvin's reluctantly extended his hands through the grating, and the cuffs were menacingly snapped in place.

******

"Where are you taking me," Calvin demanded as they pulled him from his cell for the third time and hustled him down the familiar route, but this time to a room he had never been. It was not a big room, about the size of a regular bedroom. Besides the door, the only other opening was a small window near the high ceiling. A pigeon poked its head from a nest in the little window and decided it wanted no part of what was happening and flew away. A single beam reflected a dagger-shaped shaft on the opposite wall and dimly lighted the room. Calvin's heart fluttered as he assumed a meaning to the horrid shadow on the wall. The room was devoid of furniture except for two mopping buckets in a table and three chairs. The table with the chairs was sinisterly placed in the middle of the room.

This place was as cold and unnerving as the other rooms. Just the seclusion and the meager furnishing pushed Calvin to the brink of hysteria. He was shoved inside and forced into one of the chairs.

He struggled for his life and refused to sit voluntarily. He refused to willingly give his hands be clamped. He concluded that he'll be damned if he did and damned if he didn't. There was no win in any way. He put up the struggle of his life. And at times, actually seemed to be winning. But his strength faded, and the policemen got the advantage they wanted and wrestled him into the chair and locked him in with the handcuffs.

He expected no mercy especially as he had burned his bridge. He was too angry to be terrified. He closed his eyes and promised never to beg, no matter what they threw at him, but he couldn't control that sinking feeling in his heart when the black satchel was placed before him on the table. The soft click sounded like the report from a shotgun. He couldn't restrain himself from looking, and he found it difficult to sit straight and concentrate on anything but the crude items that were deliberately extracted and placed on the table in front of him. There was a robber's black hood with an opening, six large one-way plastic straps, a notepad, and a mysteriously sealed package.

He sucked in a big draught of air. He had been holding his breath. He had no knowledge of their intention, so his mind filled in each blank. The answer was chilling. If anxiety had wings, he would have been a bird of paradise. His legs tingled, and his arms trembled. The room suddenly got small and cold. It was a coffin, and he was the candidate to be nailed in and buried alive. His body rebelled, and he had to tighten his stomach to avoid doing something terrible. He imagined the black hood closely hugging his face as it was dragged over his head, and those rigid interlocking straps… *Jesus!* he thought, *if they are tightened, they can only be released by cutting. What are they for?*

The phrase "Cowards die many times before they're dead" suited him perfectly. He was dying a piece at a time, moment by moment. He was watching his own execution. His death would be a mystery. The witnesses would be as mute as the dead. They had interred, and no one would know it was his body that was rolled out under the shield of darkness.

These bastards, he thought as his throat clogged with spit, *are cold-blooded killers*. He wondered how many innocent men were butchered at the whim of someone else. To them, they did no wrong. It was their duty and essentially a way to cleanse the world of evil men. That same evil they perpetuated.

His shouts rebounded from the walls and filled the chamber and went nowhere. Not even the pigeon returned to investigate. He twisted in his chair and strained to free his hands.

"What are you doing to me?" he croaked, and with each degree of struggle, the handcuffs ratcheted tighter until they could go no more. An ooze of blood appeared at his wrist. There it was for everyone to see, his picture in the obituary page of the *Guardian* with the shameful caption: SUICIDE VICTIM. Perhaps it would be in his best interest to admit to the crime and end the bickering. It was cowardice, but at least cowards live to tell their story and to fight another day. His pride disrupted the craziness in his mind and a small thought within said, *Good choices are never easy choices.*

"Let me out of here!" he crowed at the top of his voice. "Let me out of here!" His voice bounced back and forth against the thick wall, repeated itself and faded out. His feet were forced in place, and the black plastic straps were crudely wrapped about them and tightened to the chair. He was literally in a straitjacket.

Calvin watched with terror as the stout policeman toyed with the black hood and sashayed to the back of the chair. His short thick hands were instruments of evil. And he was chosen for this job because of his callous lack of empathy. He might have been a bouncer once ago and must have delighted in busting the head of contrary person. From the first time, Calvin saw him there was an awe for the man. Calvin knew the program had changed.

"What are you doing to me?" Calvin pleaded. He watched the death angel stalking him with his evil implement dangling playfully from his hand. Calvin closed his eyes briefly. He didn't want to see when it happened. Dying was a terrible thing. He knew it was. He had watched his friend struggle when he found out he was at the latest stage of pancreatic cancer. That thing had poisoned him and filled his eyes with jaundice. He thought he was as sound as a drum when he was at the very end of his rope. Joe didn't want to die, and he prayed and cried, and his eyes got greener, and he wasted away. A part of Calvin had died with him, and the other part was going to die at the wrong time. At least Joe was given one month's notice to get his house in order. He had none. He considered. There could only be one purpose for that hood.

"Please," he begged. "What did I do? I'll do anything you want."

The brute seized the opportunity to mark his authority with the open hand of his thick palm.

"Now you listen," he whispered with hamburger breath. "I ask the question, you answer them!" And the hood was menacingly pulled over Calvin's head. He didn't suffocate; he didn't die. The opening allowed him to breathe through his mouth.

The slow baritone gave Calvin a sense of relief that he was no longer at the mercy of his nemesis. The voice belonged to Sergeant Mullings.

"I'll ask you once again. Where is the girl?" Mullings paused and waited for an answer that he didn't receive. He continued, "You can make this easy, or make it hard on yourself. We have the evidence. You had the girl's phone in your possession. Your fingerprints are the only ones on it. We have footage of you going to the beach shortly after she did. You returned, she didn't. Come on! Fess up. What happened to her? This is your last chance."

Calvin pondered the statement. Last chance for what? He knew he was in a predicament. No matter how he answered, he would be hanged. If he refuted, he won't get out alive, and if he admitted, his execution would be delayed for another time. There were no good choices. He decided on the latter. He would not incriminate himself. His answer was emotional, but the same as before: "I don't know her, I never saw the girl."

He could sense Mullings's impatience.

"Well, if you won't speak to me, I have no choice but to hand you over to the vultures."

Mullings hung to his assertion and so did the accused. A girl was missing, and there was a suspect who had her phone in his possession. He could not deny it, but insisted that he didn't get it from her. This was incredible. He was lying! With all the marrow in his bone, Mullings knew Calvin was lying. They had to raise the temperature of their interrogation. Use extreme measures. Make him talk. He was a hardened criminal.

The chair tripped over, and Calvin's head and upper shoulders struck solidly on the tiled floor. For an instance, the officers relented and adjusted their operation. They wanted to inflict enough pain to persuade the culprit to talk, but they didn't want to leave scares or marks that might suggest that they had been physical with him. Their style of interrogation was unknown and unsanctioned by the authority, and they were willing to swear on a stack of Bibles that it didn't exist.

The contact with the floor jarred his neck and sent a painful sensation down his spine. He remained in that position, and his sneakers were loosened and pulled from his feet. He cried out aloud and waited for them to terrorize him by scratching his feet. They didn't.

Mullings hovered over the chair like a bumblebee and buzzed at the hooded head on the floor.

"Are you going to talk to me, or do I have to turn you over?"

"I've told you all I know. Do you want me to lie?" Calvin answered with his firmest voice.

He was too shocked to respond when cold water splashed over his feet and leg. It ran down his thighs and settled around his buttocks. It soaked through his trousers and drained to the floor. He now realized that the plastic pails that sat idly at the back of the room served a purpose other than janitorial service.

He was taken by surprise when the first slap with what he perceived to be a wooden paddle clapped against the sole of one foot. He thought it was another of their tactics to get his attention. He stiffened courageously and ignored the pain and waited to see what would happen next. The assault came in an outburst and rained down on both of his feet. The pain rippled and grabbed at his heel and ankle, and the soft flesh of his instep burned like he had stepped on live fire coal. It was excruciating, more than he could bear, but he could not pull away. He bawled at the top of his voice as his feet were pulverized. It was like the outer layer was pulled away, and they were beaten in a pestle like a grain crop. He lost concentration of everything except the searing pain into his feet.

Someone raised the hood and spoke close to his ear. Although Calvin was disorientated, he thought he identified the voice as that of the mean and intensive brute.

"When you're ready to talk, buddy," the voice continued, "we're ready to listen." It dropped his head with a thump on the floor.

Calvin knew that this ordeal would define his future. If he survived, he would either be confined to a wheelchair or walk with crutches for the rest of his life. And no one would believe him if he told them what happened. Every strike to his feet was a step toward his disability. The ache crawled up his calf and closed like arthritis around his knees. He cried till his voice became raucous and weak, and the muscles in his leg accepted each blow with surrender. His saliva wet his mask, bubbled in his nostrils, and dribbled back to his throat. It was like he was drowning in his spit.

He whimpered painfully. "Please don't hit me again. I'll tell you the truth. Please, I'll tell you what I know."

"If you're ready to confess, we can work," one of the beasties answered.

The beating stopped, and the chair was jolted to its upright position. He curled his toes to prevent touching the floor. The hood was spitefully pulled from his head, and he blinked distantly to try to get his focus. The lights seemed too bright for him.

Calvin's right hand was uncuffed, and the notepad that he'd seen earlier and a pen were placed in his lap.

"Listen up." Mullings was short and abrasive. "I don't have time to waste. Come clean and end this shit!"

Calvin stared blankly at the wall. He was in a different place. It was twelve years later. He was handicapped and locked up in Fox Hill Prison. He no longer cared for revenge or freedom. What haunted him was the next day. It was Sha's graduation. Instead of being there to support his daughter, he was stuck in a miserable little hole. He didn't touch the notepad. After an insidious moment, the officers realized that there would be no confession. The tablet was removed, and Calvin's hand was constrained once more.

"There you are, as stubborn as a mule." Mullings leaned so close to his prisoner that droplets of saliva sprayed annoyingly in Calvin's ear. "You will talk!" he bellowed, "You will talk or else—"

Mullings stepped to one side to allow his stout stooge to position the two pails at the front legs of the chair. His legs inclusive with the chair legs were snuff despairingly in the buckets of cold water. A fresh spasm of pain erupted in Calvin's legs and rumbled through his brain and bounced around as randomly as the ice cubes in the buckets.

The pails were positioned properly. The straps on his feet were checked and adjusted as a fire burned steadily in his sole. He was being roasted alive. The cold water was scalding hot, unbearable! He screamed in agony.

"Aaaah, aaaah! Help me! Nooo! Oh God!"

He never dreamed cold water could be so hot. He clinched his fist and wrestled in his seat and bawled until his voice became a whimper.

"We'll be back!" he heard them say as the door closed.

12

Jimmy was doubled over on a small orange crate at the stern. He felt every twitch of a bump as the fifteen-foot whaler veered through the harbor. He endured the stingy salt spray in his eyes and the pecking at the sick handlike tiny spikes of needles. The spray was persistent and burned like the caustic liniment it was, cleaning and healing and preventing the seepage of blood. It also prevented it from clotting; and in a minute, the hand was fat, red, and exaggerated. It grew into an elongate balloon with stubby fingers. One look told the story, an epic story of the struggle between a man and a crook. The man won. But the crook didn't just inflict a wound; it got the last laugh. It chewed on the palm and escaped with some prime flesh as well. The palm was left raw and hideous like it was actually chewed up and spat out in disgust. Now with the delicate markings exposed and amplified, anyone could see the large *K*. Timmy tried to hide it in his bosom, but his fingers were too big and too proud.

Bengy held the short balancing rope that was attached to the cleat in the head of the boat with one hand and used the other to wave with his shirt. He had to get some attention before they reach the mouth of the harbor. He did. His target was everyone, people in ferry boats, Jet Skis, large tenders, and those on the shore.

"Help! Help! Somebody help," he screamed, and on each occasion, the recipient gleefully returned his hail without acknowledging his peril.

He cussed the waves and swore at the air in disgust that no one seemed to understand their situation. Acknowledgement without action is no action at all. It would have been better if they didn't respond. It raised his expectations and drop him in the same breath. The skipping dinghy was given as much attention as the things that were fixed in one place. Their course was unaltered.

Anyone acquainted with Timmy could tell by the subdued and huddled figure that his spark was snuffed. He had an infectious personality that exuded confidence. He attracted all kinds of people and could persuade the devil into joining him in a pursuit. But he was now broken and a mere caricature of the man he was. With a brain, two legs, and two hands, a man could defend himself against great odds; but a loss of any limb is a tragedy to the man. There was no wonder that Timmy was miserable and dejected. His right hand, his strong hand, had parted ways with him.

He sat nursing the delicate hand in the same spot where he sat from the time they left Potters Cay. His face was strained with pain, and his vibrancy had diminished. He was quiet and annoyed at himself, like a grown man who drools in his pillow and scorns the effects. He aged on the spot. If only he could rewind everything, dismiss everything, and replay that scene again. If only he could erase failure and upload his confidence and keep it stowed on a new track. He couldn't. The hand now controlled him. A sick, unwieldy hand was his waterloo.

The boat skidded past the cruise ships at Prince George Dock, where a group of small tenders bunched together, hustling tourists to fill their quota. They scooted by Long Wharf, where people piled on the narrow strip of beach just to be near the Fish Fry, and they steered directly for Arawak Cay.

They reached the entrance to the harbor. On one side was a shallow ridge sticking out like the back of a reptile, and on the other side, hundreds of strategically placed breakwater boulders.

The whaler's speed increased as they approached the funnel-shaped passage that seemed to suck everything through in a single gulp. They tossed and dipped and skidded madly from side to side and resisted the strong current, coming miserably close to the danger spots on both sides. The passengers scrambled to stand or sit upright but soon conceded their effort. This was the infamous bar that inexperienced skippers dreaded but couldn't avoid. This was the entry and exit to Nassau Harbor. There was a constant undertow at this spot even when the water inside was as still as a pool. It respected nothing.

The skiff narrowly missed the navigation buoy marking the shallows and edged past the breakwater. Boulders added a prayer against heavy northwester. They made a sharp turn that sent Bengy clinging with both hands to the waist of the boat. Timmy fell from his crate and remained on his back waiting for better times to be reseated, his sick hand cushioned against his chest. This was the worst of the confluence, and the skiff dived in and wallowed out into the deep. They had crossed the insidious bar.

"Where in the world is this thing taking us?" Bengy howled at the wind as they escaped the rapids of the Cay. "What are we going to do?" he croaked miserably as they cleared the boundary of the land and headed into the open sea. He didn't expect an answer.

Timmy's had followed their course with great interest and, from the break, knew that this was not an ordinary fish. It had a prescribed destination, and it was resolved to take them there. He gave the best answer he could think of.

"That thing," he muttered and posed a questioned to his colleague. "Where would you go if you were hurt or in trouble?" He didn't think he had to spell out the answer. "Think about it! That's exactly where it's going."

He was right.

By now Bengy had guessed the identity of the creature, but he had never imagined a brute with such strength and tenacity to take them on such an adventure as this. He had never seen the movie or heard the story of *Moby Dick*, but it was clear he would have died many times over if he was educated about the saga. He had never seen the movie but had heard the story of *The Old Man and the Sea*, and it was a course he had no stomach for. Butterflies fluttered in his chest, and his courage sank with every wave that broke around them. His guts tumble against his ribs, and a sickly feeling gathered in his stomach. His cheek tightened, and warm drool gathered in his mouth, and before he knew it, he emptied his stomach into the sea.

Around them was a multitude of whitecaps. Ahead of them were mountainous peaks breaking and colliding dangerous. He knew it was not easy to climb over them. Behind them, the land was gradually pulling away, leaving them to the will and pleasure of the elements. There is never a good feeling being ill prepared and going into the unknown. They were led away from land for a fight that was not in their favor. The opponent set the rules for a fight that was on its turf. He watched in awe as the little whaler was lifted like a roller coaster and thrown into a wall of water that broke angrily and showered in every direction. This action was repeated over and again, and with each survival, the resilient little craft stayed afloat to climb to the next mound.

The thing was on a mission. It had maneuvered through the harbor and navigated the channels with the skill of a skipper. It had steered past every peak and valley and avoided every boulder, crack, or crevice. It knew exactly where it was going. Bengy stood in the middle of the boat in staunch disbelief, screaming and waving his T-shirt.

"Help! Help! Help! Help! Help!" he shouted until his voice cracked and his arms ached, and he managed to get a courteous hail.

He wanted to cut the cable, but with what? It was their habit to remove all implements from the boat. There was however a conch breaker that was as blunt as a sledgehammer. It would punch a hole in the boat before making a dent to stainless steel cable. He looked at the shoreline gradually slipping away and the wide circle of the horizon connecting darkly in the distance. He knew that soon they would be too far to consider abandoning ship. He weighed his inadequacy and shuddered. He had little more than a few pool lessons, and furthermore, he was convinced that his friend and mentor couldn't go the distance with a disabled hand.

What should we do? His thought rang loudly in his head and was muted by a drenching splatter of water. This was their last chance to make a ditch for it. Soon it would be impossible. He relented. Under no circumstance would he leave his friend.

Timmy must have read his mind and spoke softly, "Whatever you do, Bengy, my boy," he advised, "never leave the boat, even if it sinks."

The suggestion seemed as ridiculous as sitting calmly and willingly watching the little dinghy speeding on a course to nowhere.

The terrified beast rushed forward with the attachment in tow and made sure that the accomplice to its pain suffered proportionately. It dragged its load directly into the swells, and the flat boat got a treat from every breaker and filled up with water. The constant shower was so constant that the salty spray was no longer an irritant to their eyes and mouth.

As they diddled from wave to waves, Timmy was caught in a pickle between standing and swaying with one hand to maintain balance or with sitting on a rickety crate, sliding hazardously from side to side like an unruly piece of cargo. He concluded that standing was bad, but it was better than sitting. He stood on wobbly legs and calculated the distance and effect of every approaching wave and helplessly watched the boat fill up with water. Bengy had no alternative but to compete with the steady overflow by bailing.

The water changed from light brown to greenish blue, then to dark blue like someone had suddenly spilled an endless supply of ink all around them. And the tormented creature, feeling the freedom of the open waters, raced through the waves with renewed energy. It had to rid itself of this thing that hung on so stubbornly and tore incessantly at its throat. It tried to outrun its adversary, but the faster it went, the harder the assailant hung on. The only thing left to do was to dive and force the rascal to relinquish its hold. With blinding fright, it plunged into the abyss.

The cable hummed and scraped against the fiberglass hull and shifted from a gentle incline to a perilously steep descent that took the flat bow downward with it. Timmy forgot his injured hand and scrambled to the stern to join Bengy, who had made it there in one stride. The two men perched on the ledge of the transom, and the boat gradually stabilized and floated waist deep in the water. For the next few minutes, the swung like a pendulum high on a crest, then deep in a trough. The monster stopped and stayed at a level, the whaler squatted and waited, and the deposed joined in the salute.

The wait was short. The boat twisted and careened and scooped a few gallons of water from the side. The hull dodged down a notch and was smothered in the water as it resisted. The crew was confined at the stern as the boat ridiculously took on more water. They were alert and ready to act at the slightest change or compromise. They didn't speak. They kept their thoughts to themselves, tensed like death-row inmates, gathering strength from the fact that they had the other person's company. Emergency was written in large letters all around them: in the weather, with the monster, and the gradual weaning of the day.

They breathe freely as the boat gradually raised its shoulders and waist and drifted in the usual way.

From the position of the sun, it was almost midday, past the time when they should be sorting and distributing their cargo, not flirting precariously around on the ocean. But responsibilities and obligations were meaningless if they didn't survive. Bengy could think of nothing but the bottomless ocean and the terrible monster tearing at everything below. This encounter was different from anything he had experienced. It was much tougher than being in prison. For one thing, you generally saw your assailant, and you were never tethered to him. And if your pride wasn't too big, you could always call for help. Here, death led you where it would. His face was stamped on everything. It stared from the water, it danced on the waves, and it was ever present in your boat. There was no one to call. Even small issue of prayer was rudely interrupted by the ungracious waves.

For the first time in his life, Timmy was more worried about surviving than making another buck. The sea was his home. He had bent it and manipulated it to his advantage. He had always been the captain of his fate and master of his destiny until now. His injury had relegated to a near dependent. He rested it on his lap. The impro-vised bandage constructed by Bengy had peeled off and was hanging in the water. The hand was a major humbug and a great disadvantage to anything he had to do. He was angry at his own recklessness and cussed himself for being so careless. He was not religious, but he needed a miracle. Right now philosophy wasn't working. He sat on the ledge of the stern and whispered something to himself. He'd wel-come help from anywhere, whether natural or supernatural.

13

Although Bengy was compelled to continue bailing to keep the boat afloat, he hardly ever took his eyes from the narrow strip of the horizon. He watched the many peaks as they broke into the usual whitecaps that looked like a swarm of seagull sitting on the water. The gulls seemed to disappeared and reappeared again, and he wished he could be shared their experience. As he watched, he noticed something different. One of the whitecaps remained and seemed to increase in size. He watched it until he was convinced that it was different. When he could constrain himself no longer, he shouted, "Timmy! Timmy! Hey, Timmy!" and pointed at the horizon.

Timmy was caught dreaming and forgot he was hugging the engine and nearly tumbled off the stern. "Yes!" And his eyes followed Bengy's outstretched hand as it scanned the horizon.

Bengy dropped his hand in disappointment. He didn't see it anymore. He studied the distant rage of water with the numerous breakers and sadly said, "I'm sure I saw something. I thought it was a boat."

"It's called an illusion, my boy," Timmy responded. "Keep your eyes open for anything. You'll soon see the real one." Timmy was not critical or alarmed. It could happen to anyone. He quietly resumed his position and prepared for the oncoming swash.

"What's goin' to happen when sun sets?"

There was apprehension in Bengy's voice as he stared at the ink-black water. It was too black to see anything in clear daylight and simply thick blackness at night. And to imagine being out on the ocean at such a vile and ungodly time was just unthinkable.

"I'll tell you what, if I'm going to die, let me see my enemy and where I'm going. No sneak attacks."

To him the dark was frosty and unfriendly, and the waves were weighted with uneasiness.

"I'm sure this thing will slow down before the sun go down. It can't keep this roving for more than a day," Timmy offered. Then he continued to instruct his comrade who was green as a leaf about the sea. "Remember, if the boat sinks, hang on to it. Don't leave it, you'll be all right."

As the leader, he was accustomed to reassuring his crew, and his injury didn't change his responsibility. He had to make the hard decision even if it pained him to do so. Fear was an enemy that could be defeated. If it was allowed to run amuck, it would be your undoing.

"But in the dark, no matter what you do, the risk increases," Bengy argued.

"I know," Timmy answered thoughtfully. "The dark is a temporary inconvenience that must be addressed. Think about it, just like you move through your house when the light is out, your eyes get adjusted to the dark, and that is the time when you really use your senses. You can feel the swells, you can tell the speed and the direction of the wind, and you know when you're still or moving. We'll be okay."

He heard himself say these things but wasn't sure he believed his own words. The peaks of those waves were too high to negotiate in the dark. In a crisis, you couldn't tell whether to stay or jump. Nothing was safe or sure. They needed a streak of good.

From his cramped spot at the stern, Timmy could hear the irritable rubbing of the wire cable on the tough fiberglass bow. It was as a constant as dripping of water from a leaky faucet in a tin can or a squeaky window on a quiet night. It was annoying and a pitiful reminder of their ordeal and a compliment to the shadowy monster.

The wind picked up and came in typical November gusts with sharp jabs and quick punches. At times there was a lull for regrouping, then an onslaught of blows that could potentially knock the other fellow out if he's caught off guard. The occupants of a small craft had no choice but to be vigilant. Bengy was torn between keeping a watchful eye on the horizon and keeping the boat afloat. He couldn't afford to let another opportunity slip through his fingers and get loss in the snowy whitecaps. Then it happened. A huge wave rolled in and pushed them so high that the distant line was magnified into a big arc. The attachments deep under that was nearly always invisible was tortuously hoisted up against its will.

The boat wallowed undecidedly on a high plateau, and Bengy scanned the contour in a quick wide sweep. It yielded nothing, and his hope fell with the boat. It hardly balanced on a plain before the creature thought to make them pay for the exposure. They plunged into the breakers and once again filled up with water. Bengy's arm ached from exhaustion, but he was a machine commissioned for the purpose. He stuck it out and did his duty diligently. The last encounter had left them confused and fumbling to predict the next onslaught. They were totally surprised when the skiff bumped directly into the wind and stopped. It stopped in the path of a billow, and they were mowed over. Their worst nightmare had come true. They shared the water with their nemesis.

Bengy hardly hit the water before he was hauling himself in the boat. Timmy fell a few feet from him and flopped madly to keep his head above water. His wet jean and wounded hand were drowning him, so remained still and drifted with the wind and waves, and the distance widened. He sank unwillingly and held his breathe but still drank his fill. He remembered a technique he'd practiced as a kid—never fight the current; turn on your back and stretched out both hands and feet and float with your head above water. It worked. But he drifted away from the boat.

The creature resurfaced and turned and, at a distance, inspected the whaler. Like a miniature submarine on a covert mission, it kept a distance and collected data on its enemy. The streamlined body was camouflaged with the dark-blue water, making it almost invisible. It was a creature that carried enough dread that the mention of its name could cause a stampede on any crowded beach. It was the apex predator that knew no rival.

It glided sluggishly in the shadowy black water, perhaps resuscitating after the rugged and rigorous tussle in the deep. It seemed to be studying the object that caused the nagging pain in its neck. It pulsed slowly, and its powerful tail sent a steady revolution curling toward the boat. Its sensitive lateral lines detected a slight movement of something threshing on the surface of the water. It demanded an investigation.

Bengy was mesmerized to see the huge form waddle nearby and turned away instinctively. His friend struggled and went under and resurfaced several times, but there was nothing he could do to help him. Timmy lay still and floated with the tide.

Oh God, Bengy thought, *if there was only something to paddle with!*

He considered for a moment, then flopped down on his knees and drove his hand into the inky water and pulled forcefully back. The dinghy answered with a little bump. He repeated the act, and the boat inched forward into the wind. The curious creature moved closer to investigate as Timmy shuffled his hand to maintain floatation. The massive brute sensed the fiddling and knew the object was alive. It started a wide circuit of inquiry, which usually concluded with a predictive end. Bengy was unaware of the impending danger even though he dug deeper in the water and paddled frantically.

When Bengy saw the tailfin sticking up like a knife out of the water, he knew he had a battle on hand. This critter was indeed a brute, the most cruel and vicious animal known to man. The gruesome and horrid stories were so gut-wrenching that many of them were made into movies. *Jaws* in particular had frightened him away from the sea for months. He never wanted to face the savagery of these monsters. They had no sense but to kill. A survivor was scared for life.

The brute flanked and measured its prey and adjusting the angle of attack, and Bengy became just as incensed as the attacker. He was pumped up and shivering with fear and anxiety, and he ploughed in with all the intensity he could muster.

"I'm coming, Tim," he muttered. "Hold on, bro! I'll get you, don't give up."

Timmy was the man who had given him a second chance in life, a debt he knew was hard to repay. This was an opportunity to redeem himself and prove to everyone that he had something deep within that couldn't be written off. Timmy was the father he never had, and he was willing to give his last ounce of energy to prove it.

The skiff was almost full with water, but Bengy couldn't waste a moment on bailing. He flung his weight to one side of the boat and thrust deeply with his bare hand and pulled with all his strength. The boat slithered easily with the tide, but a monstrous wave pummeled in, and the little boat tottered drunkenly, nearly tipped over. For a split second Bengy's attention was divided between the grueling waves, his friend floundering to survive, and a mad and antagonized monster with the cable hanging from its mouth and a jarring pain deep in its throat.

The beast moved in for the kill. But Bengy, equally adept, grabbed Timothy by the collar and hauled him to the boat. Timmy was gasping for breath but managed to lift one weary leg over the side before the other was struck dead with a glancing blow. A sharp pain rushed up his leg and numbed the right side of his body, and he became immobile with the boat. The water formed a crimson belt around the skiff and followed the path of the current out to sea.

14

The room was oppressively quiet. The water in the foot pails had returned to a bearable temperature, and the searing pain in his legs had dissipated, leaving two numb lumps of flesh positioned before him. Everything happened so fast that he had no time to make good sense of the net that had closed around him. He was allowed no contact with no one: no phone calls, no legal advice, and no friendly suggestions. His family had no knowledge of his whereabouts, and his job had surgically cut him off. He was completely isolated from the outside world.

Although he was shackled, he was defiant. The interrogation was not over, and he knew it was just a matter of time before his assailants were back. They were dissatisfied with his answers. Their tactics would be woefully different and perhaps so outrageous that they defied his imagination. He didn't want to think about it. He sat rigid and resentful with his ears pricked and his eyes peering at the door expecting at any moment to see the undesirables parading down the hallway. The delay was more tormenting than the event.

The tapping of shoes was a clue that they were on their way, and his muscles tensed with anxiety. He didn't want to look like a weakling. That would embolden them to feel like he was a scary cat and an easy victim. He couldn't let them think they had broken his spirit. The footsteps stopped, and the room door opened. He pretended to be overly distracted by something that wasn't there, but their very presence affected him and his body convulsed involuntarily, exposing his deception.

Mullings strutted in, and his two goons followed.

"Well, ma boy," Mullings greeted as he walked toward his immobilized victim. "You awake?" he teased, knowing very well that anyone going through such caustic treatment would be too haunted to sleep.

Calvin didn't respond. By now he knew the cops were playing with his mind, and if he let them control his mind, they would easily control his body. He detested their ridiculous game.

Remember, speak when spoken to and answer when called, he thought as he controlled his emotions.

Mullings paced the floor and spoke as if to the other policemen.

"I said to myself, 'Calvin is a good guy. He has a wife and daughter. He lives in a good neighborhood and has a good job. He is a respectable man. He doesn't deserve this. We should treat him different.'"

The two officers answered simultaneously as if they had rehearsed for the occasion. "We agree!"

Rolle added, "That's depends on him though."

"Exactly as I thought!" Mulling added as he came to a halt in front of the wooden chair that throttled his target. "So, sir," he said pleasantly, "let's be clear about one thing. If you answer my questions honestly and be straight with me, I'll be straight with you. Let's get rid of the charade! Make it easy on yourself. You go home, and I go about my job."

Calvin did not answer. He didn't believe a single word. *You lying son of a bitch*. He breathed deeply and swallowed hard to restrain the thought. *The only good and honest policeman is a dead one*. He eyed them suspiciously, monitoring their every move.

Well, here is the question.

"Where is the girl?" Mullings kept his politeness.

This is the same-ass question again, Calvin thought and responded with guarded caution. He had been asked this same question too many times, and he had answered the same way every time. He had no other answer. He answered calmly, "I don't know nothing about no girl."

When Mullings spoke again, although he was not loud and boisterous, there was a graze of irritation in his voice.

"Come on. Before we go any further, let me tell you that we know you're linked to the girl's disappearance. We have you on tape. Maybe you're too embarrassed to tell us, so I'll give you another chance to write it."

He signaled and Rolle readily brought a notepad and pen from the satchel. The items were placed on Calvin's lap.

He looked at the gross item on his legs and wanted to toss them to hell. He could do nothing but show physical irritation. If they could see his inside, it glowed like an incinerator.

"I don't know what you talking 'bout, I mean it," he was so infuriated, his cheeks became puffy and his tears were on the verge of spilling. He could not undergo another traumatic experience. His feet were still immersed in the cold water, and the officers cagily reminded him that they were willing to deploy another horrific act.

"Those who put me in a passion will find me pipe after another fashion," Mullings quoted the line from his school days that made him sound tough. He lifted the writing material from Calvin's lap and returned them to the satchel. He held the unopened brown paper sack and toyed with it as if it were a prized item. He put the instrument on the table where there was optimum visibility. It had a hand grip and might have been mistaken for a pair of pliers if it didn't have a cup where the grip should be. The cup was like an ice-cream scoop with a strong spring. Mullings held the contraption and demonstrated how the pliers with its cup and spring worked to destroy whatever was in its range.

Calvin eyed the outrageous thing and privately questioned its use. His worry increased when an egg was positioned in the cup and the plies was cranked and released. The spring clapped back with such a sudden explosion that only his fastenings kept him in his seat. The egg shattered and spilled the residue on the floor.

The message was very clear. This diabolical tool was another horrible implement to force the toughest of men to his knees and put the fear of God in him.

Mullings approached Calvin's chair and malevolently played with the instrument. He had an impish smile on his face. Calvin waited for the question as Mullings walked to the back of his chair. He bent and whispered just loud enough for the others to hear, "Are you ready to answer me or should we proceed?"

The question was ominous. It was one that Calvin wished he didn't have to answer. There was no win. Dammed if you do, and dammed if you don't. A negative answer was terror beyond imagination. The next attack would come. Maybe his fingers, toes, lip, or nose would be mutilated. They would fall victim and be smashed, and just like the egg he would be ruined for the rest of his life. A positive answer was of no benefit. It would initiate a witch hunt that would drag him through the mud and bring nothing but harassment, heartache, and a jail cell. He was too terrified to speak. His saliva thickened and glued his tongue in one place.

Mullings thought to capitalize on the other man's stress. His strategy was working. He pressed harder.

"Take as much time as you wish to get your facts together," he intimated and led his entourage out of the room.

Like a condemned man Calvin fidgeted with his thoughts to choose a reasonable defense, but each idea seemed ridiculously insane. Admitting to the kidnapping was like shooting himself in the foot. It would eliminate his chances, and the verdict will live like a stain on his family. And the media was nobody's friend. It would have a field day eating up the story. He could think. He was up to his throat in this mire, and the more he wiggled, the deeper he sank. His head swelled and became light and groggy. It ached from ear to ear. He had to cast the die.

The key grated in the lock. They had returned too quickly. He needed more time. He watched from the corner of his eyes as the three wolves took their spot. The leader proudly walked up to him and blurted to the empty room.

"Have you made up your mind?"

Calvin hesitated as his system collapse. He felt like he needed to use the bathroom. "I need to use the toilet please," he blurted out.

"I'm sorry, ma boy," Mullings responded. "First things first. When we're done here, maybe…"

"I told you the truth," Calvin replied as the urge came on stronger. "I've never met the young lady. I don't know anything about her."

Mullings's continence fell. It was not the answer he expected. He exhaled heavily and stared with hollowed eyes. He was at his wits' end with this unpretentious liar. When he did speak, his words were riddled with sarcasm.

"So you want to play hooky poky! I'll show you what it's all about!" He stalked spitefully over to the table.

Calvin begged and pleaded his case, but the one thing he was assured of was apathy, which was the embodiment of his captors. They were so hardened that emotional displays were meaningless.

"Believe me," he implored. "Please believe me. I'm telling you the truth."

His appeal had no effect. Mullings was not about to let a bungling felon cause him to fail at the most important assignment of his career. This was a high-profile case that was entrusted to him because of his adeptness and his uncanny ability to get the job done. What was more pressing was his ambition. Promotion was at his fingertips; he was not about to let it slip away.

His subordinates were delighted in this bogeyman game and seized the opportunity to intensify the fears of their prisoner. It was like a Halloween party, the more hideous the costume, the greater the fun. They reinforced the fastening to the chair and rudely placed the awful black hood within reach. The fat bully could not restrain his insults.

"You bastards do too much shit and think you could get away with it. Not this time, buddy! Your rope just ran out."

Calvin reiterated his plea for leniency. "But I didn't do nothing."

"Shut up! You fart sack!" The fat officer pouted like a weakling who found pleasure throwing his weight around. He was as diligent as a slave to do his master's bidding.

Mullings, with toy in his hand, turned his attention to the captive.

Calvin eyed the object with awe and relived the damage it could do. He had never seen anything like it before and was confounded to death.

"What're you goin' to do with that…thing?" Calvin swore under his breath. "Not crop my fingers?" He made a fist to hide his fingers.

To deepen the intrigue, another egg was placed in the cup of the weird instrument and obliterated with a single swipe of the spring. Calvin watched with horror, not sure what to expect. He conceded that he feared the repulsively degrading gadget more than the black hood.

15

The two deckhands scrambled to the wharf as the fifteen-foot whaler dropped heavily in the water and switched around. It hustled between a hundred vessels and scooted out under its own spell. The outboard motor hanging in the water gave the stern a downward thrust that forced its head to rise so that it skipped smoothly on the water. It cleared the shallow shoal at the end of the narrows and rushed past the strong pilings of the Eastern Bridge and set a course for Arawak Cay.

Jerry sprinted through the jumble of traffic where the mail boats were loading freight for their voyage to the family islands. He got to the other side of the dock as the whaler zoomed passed with one man huddled at the stern and the other man beating the air frantically with his open hands. He couldn't hear what the man was saying, but something didn't look right. They were members of his crew, and he wanted to follow them. The whaler was their emergency dinghy that was never dispatched except on an important mission. Jerry turned to a man who was examining a load of cargo to ask for help. The man casually went about his business, and after a lengthy five minutes, he signed his work order and passed it on to his stevedore.

"Excuse me, sir," Jerry spoke urgently. "I need your help. I need to follow our dinghy. I think there's an emergency."

The man listened absently and waved at the clusters of freight stacked on the ground.

"Sorry, ma man, can't help you. Gatta get this stuff on board before midday." Not a trace of consideration was given to the other man's statement.

"But I'll pay for—" Jerry didn't have a chance to complete his statement.

"Like I say, I can't help you! It's just that simple. We're too busy." He waved his hand in the direction of a narrow three-story building enclosed with chain-link fence. "Check over there. That's the port department. That's their job."

It was as if he was hit with a stone. Jerry was dumbfounded. He had known this man for months on end. They were in the same field, mariners with an unwritten agreement to assist each other especially in distress. The exchanged of courtesies and small talks on morning after mornings meant nothing.

"I think a stingray got them," Jerry persisted as the man turned his concentration to his task.

"Are you serious?" a nearby stevedore asked in disbelief. "That stingray is probably dead by now. I can assure you it won't steal another boat after this." He giggled jokingly.

"I'm serious," echoed Jerry. "I need to use a boat to go after them."

"Now, bro," responded the mate who rejoined the conversation, "that's a different story. I don't have the authority to lend out any boat." His narrow grin seemed to trivialize the story.

"Look," Jerry tried to negotiate, "I don't mind hiring your boat."

"How much you paying?" There was a sneer in the question.

"Come on, man, let me have the boat. I'm sure Cap will pay any amount you charge." Jerry was a bit annoyed that they doubted his story.

"Sorry, bro, you'll have to wait till the big boss comes. He'll be back soon. Now if you'll excuse me, I have a ship to load." He casually dismissed his associate and walked away.

"This is an emergency!" Jerry begged, but his words were taken as seriously as the waste water spewing out of the bilge pump of a ship.

Jerry was too disappointed to think clearly. His brain was as fuzzy as a pool of muddy water. He turned to leave and was whipped with the jeering remarks of one of the men skirting around, eavesdropping on his forklift.

"Go to someone who can help, like harbor patrol? That's their building over there, and it's their obligation."

What was intended to be a joke was actually a measure of advice, and in less than five minutes, Jerry and another crew member climbed to the third floor of the white three-story building. The building had perfect visibility of the entire dock and harbor, and if anyone was watching, they would have seen the whaler skipping blindly along. They rapped on the door and were ordered in.

"Good morning, ma'am," Jerry began as they stood at the front of a long wooden counter. The walls of the room and countertop were littered with pictures of ships and important personnel, and the small office space was clustered with filing cabinets with bundles of navigation charts sitting idly atop of them. A middle-aged woman looked them over from a desk at the far back of the counter. Their courtesy was not returned, but it didn't bother them. They were accustomed to the rash ways of fishermen who preferred vulgarity over decency and only answered when it suited them. Furthermore, it was established that most government employees were discourteous and lacked the compassion and sensitivity to serve the public.

After completing her pretended scribble, the attendant remarked short and acidly as if she had been interrupted, "Yes! How can I help you?"

Jerry related his story and asked for help. There was absolute silence as the queer lady stared over the rim of her glasses and considered the question. When she did speak, her voice squeaked under her stare, "Sorry, sonny! You came to the wrong place. We don't do search and rescue!"

"But," Jerry protested, "I was told to come here for help!"

"Uh-uh!" She smiled and shook her head. "Wrong place!"

"I'll like to speak to the boss!" Jerry was flabbergasted. He felt like he was being pushed around.

"Well, well, ain't that something," the lady crowed as she got up from her roost and walked to the counter. "The boss is out, an' I'm the boss till he comes." She smiled broadly, displaying her unappreciated sense of humor.

Jerry kicked the bottom of the counter and scrambled his toes as he turned to leave. It hurt, but he didn't give a dime about it.

"Wait." The owlet glanced over her spectacles again. "Did they send you here or to the building next door? Try them," she hooted. "Green building downstairs to the right."

When they stepped out of that room, Jerry had no intention of going to a green building next door. As far as he was concerned, this was a runaround. Everyone in every office faked being too busy to help while they were actually too selfish and lazy. He was once told that to get things done, you had to be prepared to lick someone's boots or to provide some incentives.

I'll be damned, he thought. *I'm not licking nobody boots, and I ain't paying no one to do his job.*

It was frustrating to think that people created reasons for delays. Good attitude was everything; it determined where you would live and certainly how you would die.

He looked at the white metal door as they left and wanted to give it another kick; the stinging in his boots prevented him. He tweaked his courage and crawled downstairs and looked around indecisively. Fifty feet away, a large olive-green sign in all caps painted on white background read, "Royal Bahamas Defense Force." Was it worth the effort to check them out? He was fed up with all the negative vibes that everyone gave.

The door was open, and Jerry and his companion found themselves once again standing at the front of a large counter with two officers stationed in the wide back area. They were both absorbed in the latest editorial of the *Punch*, catching up on the latest gossip from the Nassau grapevine. Jerry's first impulse was to turn and walk out. They faced the same thing again—nonchalance. His friend read his mind and held him by the elbow and urged him to stay. The officers stayed where they were and made it clear who were in charge there.

Jerry whispered under his breath, "These snotty nose sons-a-bitches supposed to be serving the public!"

There was a familiar saying that only two things spurred them to action, drugs and firearm, and this complaint didn't match any of them. He waited.

One officer raised his head from the paper and asked sarcastically, "What's the problem?"

Jerry wanted to say, "Sucker, you're the problem. You're too busy in other people's shit." He stifled the urge and stated calmly, "I have an emergency…" And he related the story for the third time.

"So what do you want us to do?" asked the officer carelessly as if the problem was not obvious.

"I need your help in going after Cap and Bengy. They must have gone far by now."

The officer handed a plain sheet of paper and a pen to Jerry and told him to write a statement explaining what happened. This was the ultimate challenge. As a boy, Jerry attended school when the weather was too bad to go fishing, and after sweltering patience, one of his colleagues gave up trying to teach him to read. He was proud he could scribble his name. He explained his shortcoming and begged the officer's indulgence.

"What time did this incident occur?"

"Where did it take place?"

"Who were involved?"

"Why did you wait so late to report it?"

Jerry was relieved when it was done. He made his atrocious mark at the bottom of the page and left.

16

The two cronies knelt on the floor and held the petrified prisoner and started to undo his belt. Mullings stood a little distance away, fingering the weird contraption and appallingly crushed another egg to illustrate the savagery of the instrument. Calvin's eyes widened with terror, and his mind tripped and fell on the lasting damage the thing would do to his spirit and his physical acceptance. He didn't want to believe his mind.

No way! They can't do that to me, his thoughts slipped out involuntarily. "No! No! No!" he bawled loudly and stiffened his legs to prevent them from removing his trousers.

"Nooo!" he yelled again and again and lowered his head to see what was really going on. He pressed his buttocks firmly against the chair and squealed like a pig as his trousers were dragged below his hips, then over his thighs and below his knees. Except for his underpants, he was all but naked. He understood the full implication of the egg experiment, and as Mullings deviously advanced, he felt the cold dark steel touching his skin and aiming for the delicate part of his private part. There was no question about it. The contractile muscle would not hold up under such stress. It was not designed for pressure and could never withstand the rigidity of that violent spring.

He remembered a soccer game where he was laid out from a glancing kick in the groin. He doubled over on the grass, rolling with pain as the ref rebuked his opponent for unsportsmanlike conduct and issued him a personal foul. It was a serious thing to intentionally, or unintentionally, invade a man's privacy. He was now committed to the very same indignity.

The veins on his neck and forehead stuck out like ropes as he gripped the handle of the chair and yelled like his lungs were bursting.

"Pleeeease! Nooo!"

Mullings was unmoved by the blubbering of his hostage. He was loving every moment of this escapade. He remained calm as he fidgeted his vile toy. He was confident that he would draw out a voluminous confession.

"Do you wish to talk to me now, or do you need more convincing?" he asked.

Calvin was hysterical and saw that these men would spare nothing to have their way. His mind was as blank as an unused sheet of paper. He had to say something to satisfy his godless, unhinged outlaws. Whimpering alone would not save him. He was that child waiting to be walloped for breaking a sacred rule. Apprehension closed in as Officer Rolle stalked him on one side with the appalling hood and on the other side Officer Mullings edged closer with his fiendish tool. His head was snapped upward and hooded, and he lost sight of the encircling evil that he wanted to keep an eye on. His heart pound relentlessly at his temple and his legs convulsed at the touch of the cold disgusting item on his thigh.

"Please don't!" he yowled like a suffocating wolf. Then he whimpered passionately, "I'll do anything you want! Please don't!" His muffled remarks would have moved anyone besides his adversary.

"Oh no! no! no! no!" His words came in short gasps as gritty fingers pulled at the waistband of his boxers. He clawed down on the chair and curled his toes in protest. He knew what was going to happen. The veins bulged again on his neck, and a pounding pain returned to his temple. He blurted a thunderous scream, "Ooom! Ooom!"

The room went quiet, and his head drooped to his chest like a wilted leaf.

17

For a few harrowing minutes, Timmy was caught in a tug-of-war between his friend and a formidable beast with an unquenchable lust for blood. And Bengy was willing to risk his life to show what true loyalty meant. One of Timmy's legs was locked in the powerful jaws of the critter that dished out nothing in return for service except pain and anguish. It showed no mercy and had no friends. The bargain was clear—cut, kill, and eat. Even if it wanted to suspend its rage, an internal drive from deep within said no and propelled it to clean up every wisp of blood and remove every residue of flesh. At the scent of blood, all other functions and impulses were suspended, and pain and exhaustion were transformed to energy. Blood was irresistible.

The torpedo head rose above the wave with its mouth full, which blocked the precious saltwater that flowed through the narrow slits at the side of its head. Right now personal peril was meaningless. There was a bigger focus. The monster shook violently and tried to decimate its victim.

"Oh, gawd!" Timmy bawled and latched to the side of the boat. The veins on his neck and arm bulged like strands of rope. "Please don't let it get me!" he bawled desperately. "Pleaseee," he wailed until his words faded in his throat. He couldn't remember ever begging for anything before, but this time was different. The cord of life seemed more brittle than before.

Every bone in Bengy's body rebelled. His head ached, and he shook like a leaf in hurricane. The stress of the moment took complete control. His hands trembled as he gripped the wet clothing that was part of the human being that begged for help. He was too nervous to hold on but too scared to let go. He was equally as terrified as the individual that was impaled between millions of spikes. His teeth chattered, and he bit down on his lip to control his anxiety. His mouth filled up with spit. He swallowed and realized that it was thick and different from the salt water.

He had seen it before. It happened a few weeks ago and haunted him like a ghost from the macabre. The frail derisive being had come again. Bengy painfully recounted the last challenge. The dark resolute figure operated in two dimensions: black or white; live or die.

It returned to him like it was yesterday. On that occasion, he had forgotten to adjust the exhaust control on his diving apparatus, and instead of pumping pure oxygen to the diver, he fed him a toxic batch of carbon monoxide. The diver passed out.

Bengy watched as the ocean gradually turned the body over and left it to float face up with outstretched hands like a single-engine aircraft. Death gave a solemn approval, and Bengy kicked the hose in disgust. The unconscious body floated effortlessly to the surface. What happened was textbook affair. The diver was rushed to the mother ship and surrounded with thick, dry blankets and given CPR.

Bengy knelt at the side of the victim. His words welled up as he spoke.

"Come on, Bruno. You can't leave me like this."

He got no response.

The captain cordially wrapped Bengy in a bear hug.

"Don't you worry, my good man. You did the best you could."

Death waited at a step away and malevolently smiled as the exhausted crew gave up. In despair, one of them dropped a bucket over the side of the boat and pulled it up with water. He doused the prostrated figure and tossed the bucket away. The body jerked and convulsed at the contact with water. The dead man coughed several times and sucked a breath of fresh air. They had cheated death.

He had seen it all, and the visuals floated back again and again like scenes from a horror movie. Here was an episode of a spearfishing trip. He was tapped with the pleasant task of operating the boat for a diver. The water was choppy and muddy, but the diver insisted on going down. It was only thirty feet of water, but Bengy could scarcely see the bottom. Moments after the diver jumped overboard, Bengy noticed the compressor hose floating horizontal on the water. This was a bad omen. The hose is always attached to the diver. But there was no diver. He used his water glass and took a quick sight through the dregs at the bottom. No diver. Then he heard a muffle voice like someone starving for air and saw a head bobbing in the distance. Bengy rushed over to find the man weakly treading water with one hand and fighting against the wind and current that gradually dragged him away. The pale-orange water explained what had happened. His right shoulder and upper arm were tattooed with punctures, and his mangled elbow and lower arm hung loosely like a temptation to a hungry villain. The diver was bleeding profusely and passed out before he was taken in the boat. The monster sliced the water in a frenzy, searching for the morsel that had alluded him.

But nothing compared to this demon that gave him the fit of a struggle. His grip on the wet fabric was slowly slipping away, and he knew a few more headbutts and jolt or two were enough to wrest his partner away. Bengy hung on, and the brute stood its ground. He thought about tug-of-war and playing possum, relaxing and catching the opponent off guard, and concluded that it won't work. It would give the adversary more leverage to set its razor-sharp incisors and rip through arteries, sinews, and maybe bones as well. He hung on like he was hanging on for his own life.

He noticed a rusty conch breaker sitting in the bottom of the boat. It was the only weapon available and hardly a weapon with which to go battle. He grabbed it by the stubble handle and poured out his madness on the unwary quarry.

"Brute! Brute! Brute! Brute!" he screamed in a fit and jabbed with all his might. He held on with one hand and punched with the other. Something snapped and balked like a zipper failing under stress. He continued his assault on the bullet head, and the zipping sound increased, and the rigid blue-jeans flagged in the water and ripped free. The creature was still driven by its three small senses: detect, engage, and eat. One urge was unfilled. With the swish of the head, it latched on to its prey and ignored the pain smashing through its skull. The short handle of the mallet was soon plastered with blood and slime and slipped indignantly and twiddled out of sight. For a hairy moment, his hand twisted and pried awkwardly away as the monster gave a desperate shake that would have dislodged any hamstring. Instead, the hollow leg of the trousers swathed the creature like a bandage, covering both eyes and mouth. This new thing brought the old fight to an abrupt ending. The stupefied animal swashed its head franticly from side to side to detach itself and rushed blindly in the misty water.

The little craft became cranky with its overload of water. It sat at a mere six inches from being swallowed up. It squatted and wallowed despairingly, and just when its passengers thought they had seen its last, it rose like a Jet Ski and conquered the next wave. A haggard and beaten man lay in the hollow of the boat with the cold, dead water splashing savagely against his wound. He lay on his back, rolling to the motion of the boat. Both hands clamped about the knees, trying to do the greatest good to the sickest limb. He grimaced in pain but offered no resistance as the saltwater washed over his wound and added to the sickly discoloration that flowed freely into his eyes and mouth. He drank the grimy stuff and choked and hiccupped on his own blood. His tough pair of jeans was now a one tawny leg end, snagged short during the fight. He was beaten, broken, and bleeding but still alive.

Bengy desperately wanted to help, but he had the rickety boat full of water to contend with or face the fatal wrath of the open sea.

The vengeful creature instinctively returned to its course with a battered head, a steel cable still ringing in its jaws, and the remnant of a frisking blue fabric laced over its eyes. The boat scuttled sluggishly and remained more congruent with the ocean than a safe spot. Bengy was overcome by the tremendous amount of bailing he had to do to offset the deluge that seemed to come from everywhere. He watched his companion hug his leg and rolled from side to side in the bloody water and wished he could do something to ease his pain, but the waves were too erratic, and he knew that an errant twist or an unnoticed attack could be a catastrophe. At times, Timmy's swollen hand was his undoing. He had very little control of it, and it became a hazard to itself. At every toss or turn, the hand got in the way and baited Timmy to try to do something about it. The result was regrettable.

Bengy ditched the stagnant water overboard and paused in between to see if by chance some miraculous favor was extended to them. But the deep troughs and breaking waves quickly erased the presence of the flat boat. Eventually, he found the courage to do the very thing that terrified him.

Timmy lay shivering in the dead water in the boat as the chilly wind bite against his half-naked body. His energy waned, and he felt dizzy. The bright sunshine did not change the fact that it was November and close to the start of winter. His muscles tightened, and his pain became so intense that he coiled into a knot to warm himself. He closed his eyes to erase the gloom and hostility that had taken control of his life. The stained bandage that once covered his swollen hand hung like a discarded rag. He thought of unwinding the wrapping to provide dressing for his stricken leg, but the hands that wrapped his knee also brought a degree of comfort. He was pitifully losing vibrancy and was becoming disabled. The diluted bloody water continued to splash in his face, and he closed his mouth and timed his breathing to prevent drinking. Bengy scooped up the water and tossed it overboard. Neither of the men spoke. Their thoughts communicated at a different level. He ditched the repulsive water overboard and watched it disappear into the surf.

*****

The day wore on, and the wind picked up, and the whaler wobbled and skidded callously with its passengers tucked in like wayfarers from a refugee camp. At one moment, a lift of waves or something in the distance brought renewed hope. At other times, that little spark was rudely dashed aside to reveal an extensive dark ocean. Timmy sat in a huddle to build up his body temperature while Bengy dug into keep the skiff as dry as possible. He continued to watch the wide expanse of the horizon for any aspiring sign. In front of them, the wide ocean spread out like a huge landscape with a range of rugged peaks. Some of these peaks were too far away to assume their treachery, and others were close but too craggy and dangerous to conquer. They rose high up at one moment, then unsuspectingly flattened into an endless plateau. Bengy wondered who would venture out in such a turbid and inclement weather. His answer came quickly as a drove of seagulls screamed at him and sat amidst the turbulent waves.

Although he had been burned so many times in his youth, Bengy had never felt so helpless and so much like an imbecilic as he did right now. His journey to this point was far from being a bed of roses. As a youth, he had to navigate through hundreds of indiscretions and ramble through a maze of bad habits, some of which landed him in the pit. He had to put up and shut up when he smelled others fart or emptied their slop bucket. The street was his sanctuary, and the block, his university. He could face the most ruthless convict and predict his intention long before it was executed. But today his opponent was different. She was shifty and smart and played on his nerves, inventing the rules for the game as they played. The chance of winning was slim, and losers paid with their life.

The sun slipped passed its zenith and hid under a bundle of thick clouds and left Bengy just as gloomy as the shade on the waters. The night was here, perhaps moment away, and Bengy decried its approach. There is no price for being in the dark. His sin had landed him there. The sin of bellicose and rebellion. The darkness was his home for fourteen days. It remained his enemy. The dark was unpleasant and corrupt. It exposed his weakness. Of course, he cried and allowed his enemy to dance on his head. He was fed tack through a cubbyhole and was never sure whether he'd have a meal or be a meal. He detested the dark. It was confinement. A six-by-eight space with you and your commode. You'll never forget the smell of shit for the rest of your life. Some call it solitary confinement. I call it hell—dark hell. You eat in the dark, and every night, you go to the gallows with your head in a bag.

Bengy's muscles tightened, then relaxed when he saw the serenity on the face of his handicapped friend. He had reasons to be bitter, but he wasn't. The scrawl rolled away from Bengy's face.

"Ben, just remember if your opponent is stronger, use his strength to your advantage. Wisdom will defeat strength any day."

Bengy smiled confidently. There was yet a bright spark to this confinement.

18

$\mathcal{B}$engy had been looking at the horizon for so long that his eyes grew tired and drew everything together so that they began to look alike. His eyes were constantly filled with water, but he could not tell the difference between tears or the salty spray that singed the tender muscular lining. The thick cloud that once shaded the sun dropped near to the surface and floated across in a mild tropic that peppered the waves with heavy droplets that bleached them free from salt. Before the shower disappeared, Bengy was back at his chore, bailing fervently and searching the horizon desperately for help.

At one instant, the whaler was hemmed in a tunnel, then ditched unnervingly toward the steep incline of another gigantic wave that hesitated and flattened and stayed just long enough to allow for a scan of the horizon. Then the mountain shattered, and everything plunged downward to repeat the maneuver all over again. It was hard to get use to such a dizzying exchange, and his guts tumbled and retched like he had plunged fifty feet from the sky. But as unnerving as it was, it gave him a clear view of the extremity and allowed him to read the differences between ruffs and ridges. It was on one of these rugged missions that something different appeared in the breakers at the bottom of a bubble of clouds. It was too small to be a waterspout and too constant to be a whitecap. Before he could make a guaranteed assessment, it leaped on the spot and disappeared as he was swallowed by the next big wave.

"Help! Help! Over here! Over here!" he shouted, and his voice was lost in the wind and waves that were tearing and fighting at each other. Nobody heard him, and nobody saw the flat skiff snuggled so deep in the water that she could hardly be depicted as a line in an artist review. Bengy stood on the narrow headboard and held the bow rope to secure his balance. But standing was of no consequence. It made no difference. His lean, brown body blended perfectly with the distance and became one with the ocean. He watched in dismay as the speed boat clapped despairingly and raced toward the shadow of the land.

"Over here," he barked and waved his hand until he lost his footing and tottered and tipped on one foot until he reclaimed his stance. "It passed me! Oh no! No! No! That son of a…"

The rest of the word was lost in the yowl of a wolf on the prowl. He looked around for something to strike or kick to get his emotion out. There was nothing. He was crushed and stampeded on the spot and missed his footing again and nearly fell overboard.

"That fricking good-for-nothing thing just jingled past and went out of sight! They were so close." He measured between his hands. "I could spit on them, but they didn't bat an eye this way!" He was very irate. "I'm sure they saw us! But they passed! Ahhhaaa!" he screamed like the Incredible Hulk, without a shirt to tear away. He ranted with rage and released his frustrations in the surges.

*****

Bengy's felt like someone had turned him upside down like a piggy bank and had shaken everything out him. He had nothing in him. He was worthless. He couldn't stop a passing boat even though it was close enough to piss on. He was no smarter than a schoolyard bully, a bellow man with a big mouth with no substance. He skulked despondently at the head of the boat, booing himself, silently wondering what exactly was going on in that silent skull at the back of the boat, except pain. He scooped up a handful of water and swallowed it. His stomach rebelled with a hungry growl, and he burped aloud. He remembered that he had neither eaten nor drunk anything since the night before; and now that he thought of it, he realized that his throat was parched and gritty, his lips were charred and sore, and he was as hungry as the shark they were following. He licked his blistered lips to get rid of the stinging salt, and he sank deeper in despair.

Timmy was coiled up near the stern of the boat, weaving through the pain and grief that he couldn't denounce. He was saddled with worries, but he was not one to show them. He understood that just talking saps the waning energy. He hardly spoke.

"Hey, Cap, you awake?" Bengy called as a large wave rushed in and seemed to knock the platform from under his feet.

Timmy opened his eyes briefly and mumbled inaudibly, "Can't hear you."

Bengy responded, "How you feel?" He felt ashamed to ask 'cause the answer should be most obvious. He didn't need an answer. "Could do with a drink of water and a crack conch. How 'bout you?"

The remark caused Timmy to tweak his meager reserve and answer, "All you do, don't drink that seawater," he muttered.

"What's wrong with it?" Bengy inquired. "Water is water, and it's nice and cool. Is this one o' them fairy tales that says, 'Water, water everywhere and not a drop to drink'?"

"Listen, my brother," Timmy continued. "If you drink that water, you'll wish you'd met your Maker an hour ago. You'll be sicker than a dog."

Bengy didn't understand the pretext, but he stayed from the water.

The waves beat stubbornly against the boat without changing her speed or altering her course, and the land disappeared and left them in the middle of a moving circle of hills and valleys. Bengy stared at the oval-shaped distance and the broad flatness that marked complete isolation. It was like the boat was sitting on a large plate with a rugged rim somewhere out there that was ready to suck someone over the edge, but if you survived that, there was that large blue dome that locked you in and prevented an escape. This was not complicated science. Even a mushy brain could figure that out. The devil's triangle was real, and the earth was flat. Now how far it was before you reached the edge of the ring was another question.

He sat, and the boat thumped and galled him in his seat and forced him to stand and ride on unsteady feet. He stared outward and tried to imagine the seething horrors that could be lurking in the distant mounds, which would definitely come out after dark. The ocean shifted with his vision between the sky and sea so rapidity that sometimes he thought he was watching the sea when he was actually looking at the sky. Like staring in a river, it takes forever to figure out that what you see is not the sky but a reflection. This reaction capitalizes on the hungry and weary. It mirrors your desire and appears as thing that brings gratification. If you fall for it, you're hooked. It may cause your death.

Every breaker became alive with something that didn't exist. Bengy pinched himself and focused on the one thing he wanted to sea—a boat.

A big wave approached, and Bengy was forced to use his seaman's legs to ride it out. Like others, it rose high and intimidatingly, pulling the horizon into focus as with a magnifying glass. The whitecaps pranced in the distance and ran to join the leg of clouds at the lip of the curve. Bengy followed the rim as fast as he could to be ready for the preceding huge swell. For a split second, he didn't pay attention to the water collecting in the boat and only realize that they were all but swamped when the whaler struggled forever to get out the trough and climb to the top of the next roller. Bengy had a decision to make, ignore flooded boat or ignore the sight that comes with the next breaker. He chose the latter.

Another mountainous wave came in and rough them up and demonstrate who was in charge. They went with the flow; they had no choice. But they decided to make lemonade with the lemons they were given, the large wave that grabbed them and surged upward. As they crested, his eyes filtered the content of the bend, and he noticed something he'd missed or something he hadn't seen before: a small object popped into view and disappeared. He maintained his focus, and the tiny object bobbed into view again. And before he could give it credence, their time was up, and the little dinghy plunged into a valley between the waves.

As much as he dreaded the heights on nothing but water and the calamitous tumble in a watery hole, he was anxious for another scary ascent. He bowed his legs and planted his feet on the bow and waited. A massive wave came as predicted and took him on the terrifying journey to the top of the clustered peak. He recognized his blob and froze on the spot. He fastened his eyes on the object, and his eyes found the minute blob. He didn't dare to wink. The particle grew rapidly and moved quickly within scope. He remembered the opportunity that had slipped away and swore it would never happen again.

The whaler dipped precariously, and Bengy went skipping along the narrow waist like a tightrope walker. There was nothing to cling to. If he lost his balance, the wide sea would salute him in the most disrespectful way. He steadied himself like an astronaut who had braved one adventure and was up to the challenge to take on another.

"Oh Lord, please don't let them pass us!" he whispered. Or did he pray. He had stopped praying a long time ago. God was seldom there when you needed Him. Did he repent? Was he now convinced that only God could help them? "Lord! Don't let them pass us," he repeated as the little boat rose high on a plain, and he could to see the wafting outline coming their way. A curdling scream escaped his throat.

He held the short bow rope and jumped for joy and waved his hand and shouted.

"Here! Here! Here! Over here!" He waved nervously and screamed at the craft as it skipped into view.

Timmy remained in his position and showed no emotion. It was difficult to tell whether he was elated or didn't care. One thing was, he continued to hug his knee and whimper like a sick animal.

Bengy's heart fell pounded, and he was as nervous as a child who wanted his present before Christmas.

"Over here! Over here! Over here!" Bengy shouted at the top of his voice.

The boat came near, and he could see its color and see the heavy waves splashing in plumes over the sides. He could see its registration number, too smudged to identify but clear enough that it was there.

"Hey, Timmy! Timmy," Bengy ignored their peril and went and shook the unresponsive shoulder to share the good news.

Timmy groaned in acknowledgment and slightly raised his head from the huddle of his knees.

"Uuh ha! Uh ha."

"Timmy, a boat's here! They're here," Bengy repeated.

Timmy rolled his eyes and frowned from the huddle of his knees.

19

B engy was wound up like a spring and was too tense to stand, but there was no place to sit. He knelt in the water and clasped his hands together and reached for the sky in a symbol of gratitude. He stood trembling and unconsciously hung to the short bow rope, his brown body wet and glossy like he'd been baptized in oil. He hardly noticed the chilly wind on his naked body and the salty spray that kept him licking his lips to sooth them. The thirty-foot black-and-orange *Zodiac* throttled down at a safe distance away and assessed the scene, then slowly maneuvered toward the submerged craft. They were told about the two men. One was standing, but where was the other? It took a while to determine that the huddled object at the stern of the boat was the other person they were looking for.

Bengy was elated. "Thank you! Oh, thank you!" He wanted to relate the entire ordeal in one sentence. "Cap got bite and is bleeding to death! Oh Lord, please help me! Help me! He can't move!"

His words rang over the waves, and he pointed to the wretched bundle submersed in the skiff half filled with the nasty red water. It was evident that something was wrong. The crew of the *Zodiac* could not see the taut cable extended outward to the shadowy object hidden by the waves, but they knew something was wrong. The boat was making way out to sea with a frantic man on the bow and a lifeless package rolling in a boat filled with water.

In his uneasiness, Bengy had forgotten to bail. The boat was swaying clumsily, and although Timmy didn't complain, he was so cold that his teeth chattered. Bengy collected his bailing apparatus and tossed the water out and refitted his jeans around his injured friend. The whaler slowed and stopped and turned abruptly as if the usurper was about to challenge the follower. A dark shadow sailed to the spot where the bloodied water was ditched overboard. This was not their assailant. It was too small, extremely aggressive, and didn't have a battered head or a steel cable hanging from its mouth. It raced through the sullied water and rammed blindly into the side of the sunken skiff as it collected particles of clotted blood.

The wire cable went slack, and they noticed a larger shape inching like a distressed submarine toward the vulnerable craft. It moved without a ripple and was hardly detectable. It sniffed the bloody deposit and saw the intruder. It was not wearing the bandage across its face, and it was hard to detect injury to its head. The powerful tailfin pulsed with indignation, and the unwelcomed guest quickly vanished.

The crew of the rubber craft saw the adversary and the attachment in the head of the whaler and quickly formulated a plan. If they freed the monster, then concentrate on the rescue, there was no guarantee that the deranged creature would simply go away. And even if it did leave, the contraption in its mouth would limit its ability to hunt and may cause it to seek an easy human prey.

The critter passed a few feet from the rubber craft and studied it and turned aside. It was not the foe. It began circling the whaler with renewed enthusiasm like it was casting a web around it. The cable hitched around the prop of the outboard engine and created a fresh set of tension. The pestered creature splashed frantically in a circle with the whaler in tow. The terrifying display sent one marine racing out of sight to return with a loaded harpoon and a coil of nylon rope. The pilot nodded silently in approval. The loose end of the rope was secured to a cleat in the bow of the rubber craft, and the marine waited for the critter to move in position, clear of the distressed craft. The harpoon whizzed through the air like a missile with the yellow nylon rope trailing behind it. It struck with a thud, penetrating the tough, gritty skin and gripping firmly into the sinewy flesh.

The distraught animal zipped out of sight, leaving a gurgling whirlpool and taking the whaler sternward out of sight. Bengy impulsively leaped from the incline boat and hustled to assist his friend who was tossed like a doll in the turbulence. With on hand tucked firmly under his shoulders and the other still clutching the bow rope, he pulled forward with all his strength. He felt the tension of the downward spiral and released the rope as the bow slipped beneath the surf. Bengy was not leaving his friend. Together they had survived the trauma of an angry ocean, and he had single-handedly snatched him from the jaws of death. Like a gallant soldier, he would not leave his fallen comrade on the battlefield. He promised they would die together.

To a seasoned swimmer, fifty feet was a few strokes away, but to the novice, it was as traumatizing mile. And it was especially tantalizing when somewhere in the abyss was a monster who hated your guts, striving furiously, tearing at anything to settle a score. It was a dreaded adversary. Bengy knew his limitations, but he was not leaving his friend. He flapped about as his uncontrollable weight pulled him under, and he drank his fill. There was no opportunity for a second lesson, and this was not the middle of a swimming pool that allowed you to stand at will. His load was a humbug. He had moved less than ten feet but was already out of air. He sank, and his chest expanded to bursting point. It was a struggle to keep his head up, but he refused to relinquish his load. He felt a furtively kicking that pushed them back to the surface and knew they were propelled by a power that wasn't his own.

Bengy splashed and struggled and drank excessively and began to lose orientation. His forearms became sluggish and unwieldy, his legs were like boulders weighing him down, and his chest felt like it would explode for lack of air. He had bitten off more than he could chew. He never thought death by drowning was so painful and hard. And there was nothing he could do about it. He was sinking in a place of despair. He eyes lost focus as he reached a wide plain of darkness. He sensed a movement beside him. He had no fear, no care, and no clue of anything. His adversary no longer existed. His body shot to the top. His eyes opened, his head swung back, and his mouth opened wide and drank the air in big gulps. He floated effortlessly with head and shoulders above the water. It took him a minute to realize that there was a man beside him, and he was supported by floating device stuck around his body and under his shoulders. As he acclimated, he looked franticly around, and to his relief, he saw a small raft moved gingerly on the bumpy waves. It was carrying a bundle that was easy to recognize. He relaxed for the first time for that day. He might not have collected wrinkles, but he surely had grown old. This single day felt like a lifetime.

Bengy didn't need direction. He paddled nervously for the rubber craft. They had cheated death again.

20

The beast ranted defiantly with the cable sawing between its teeth, the harpoon boring firmly into its back, and the buoyancy of the whaler forcing it to return to the surface. But even a mortal wound could not change the firm instinct that was embedded in its system. The desire to hunt and kill was as near as the next splatter of blood, and this drive was stirred and reinforced by fishermen at Potter's Cay who absentmindedly dumped buckets of slush in the sea every morning. They wetted the appetite and summons the creature to another journey to scavenge or kill anything in its path. And the voracious hunter set out and left nothing in its path. Not even a piece of rag or an old glove caught up in the mix of food was spared its avarice.

On this rendezvous, the water was murky, and the sun was just creeping in to begin the day. But this creature did not rely on sight to navigate. The pebble-size brain could detect a drop of blood in turbulence a mile away, and although its marble eyes resisted the diffusion of light, its sensory receptors and lateral lines were as efficient as the radar of a nuclear submarine. Once the creature had zigzagged to within fifteen feet of its victim, its receptors zoomed it in and it struck with deadly precision. It was an acute headache to the unsuspecting venturer and a deadly killer to the careless perpetrators.

Today the scent of blood was strong, and the course was zeroed in for its destination. The tide was at a strong ebb, with the current rushing westerly at a steady five miles per hour. This torrid pace was daunting for even the best of swimmers. But the impulse was convincing and too appealing to resist. So the solitary hunter pushed through heavy traffic, avoiding contacts and collecting and refining all data to justify its course. Nothing could deter it, not even the speeding crafts that sliced through the water and missed it by mere inches or the heavily laden tenders that drove with such tyrannical force that their sheer momentum have broken down bridges. Nothing, nothing could apprehend it including the never-ending persistent current that flattened the seabed, pushing in the opposite direction. This was his territory, and he controlled it with vigilance. Stragglers were unwelcomed, food was plentiful, and the competition was moot.

Without changing speed, it examined everything in its path: a bundle of straws drifting callously, a submerged plastic bucket, a loose car tire bouncing up and down on the waves, a camouflaged log drifting horizontally between wind and water. Each received due attention and was deferred as useless riffraff.

Somewhere in the distance, a vibration was detected. The dull vision tried to focus on the object that was flapping and flailing like a big fish in a net. The thing had a strange odor, not that strident fishy smell that demanded a confrontation, and there was no blood. At first, the monster deferred a strike in search of more tasteful game, but the incessant twisting and grabbing at the waves was too tempting to resist. The brute zigzagged to determine the line of scrimmage, narrowed the zone of attack, and zeroed in for the kill. At ten feet away, it shot out like an arrow and struck the quarry. Blood gushed, and the victim thrashed aimlessly and offered up little resistance. The blood clouded the figure and infused the monster with excitement. An insatiable urge blotted out all reasoning and awareness. The beast shook free of the contraption and made a quick decisive circle to collect its bearing. It was spellbound and became agitated. Each strike became more deadly than the other. In the profusion, the brute grabbed a mouthful of the spoil, a combination of clothing and flesh, and shook violently to dislodge it from the prey. The bright-red blood gushed for a moment then oozed to a trickle and became one with the ebbing tide. The assailant was satisfied with its performance, redirected its course, and rescinded the hunt for the day.

21

The terrified monster dug deep to find a way to escape, creating a vortex with its descent. It was attached to something that defied all tricks or trifles and refused to let go. The deeper the monster went, the firmer the thing held on and tried to pull it back to the surface. Fear was changed to panic, and panic became the only avenue to struggle live and escape. But buoyancy closed the door of escape and denied even another inch of depth. And the sturdy harpoon with its extension wrenched and twisted and ripped at the muscular sinews and opened a hole in its back. The shock was unbearable, and the pain was excruciating as the large cavity filled up with water and exhaustion dragged it to the surface. The shimmering white outline of the whaler came into view and settled like a bathtub rimming with water. The little engine was still attached to the stern but was beaten and worn and had lost its cap.

The crew of the *Zodiac* knew the creature would emerge at any time and prepared and waited for the attack.

They maneuvered in position and stalked the man-eater like the predator it was. They were determined to waste it in the same way it had wasted so many of its victims. After what seemed an endless wait, the elongated body broke the surface and pushed forward for the open sea with all of its load, which had doubled under tow. It made no haste but defied the odds of stopping and plodded into the wind, pumping with renewed vigor.

"I think we've got him this time," the pilot said as they edged forward to get in line with the streamline shape.

"It will soon run out of energy. It has no swim bladder and must continue swimming to stay afloat."

Bengy smiled at the remark and spoke for the first time since being rescued.

"This one doesn't get tired. It must be from hell itself. It's been swimming all day."

This adventure was an ordeal. The creature was accustomed to hunting around shallow shoals and coastal areas but never in the deep tussling with the forceful flotation of well-crafts and the suck and draw of mountainous waves. The flight slowed to a waddle, the nylon rope slackened and floated on the water, and the marine braced against the side of the boat and leveled his rifle at the victim. There was a short pop and a kick and a splitting of the surface like a stone skipping on a lake. He missed. He didn't account for the boats tossing on the waves. The marine positioned for a next shot. This time he counted the waves and waited for the break that comes after the fifth surge.

"One...two...three...four...five...pop!"

The explosion was small but effective. The sea swirled, and the cable sang and got taut as the whaler gathered speed and the yellow rope stretched like a rubber band and the harpoon that was embedded in the back of the enemy came whizzing back and sank with a thud into the upper lip of the *Zodiac*. The spear dug into the sturdy molding, and it hissed and whistled and slowly flattened. The distraught beast plunged downward but instantly floated in a torrent of froth and bubbles. The shattered head grinned menacingly under a couple of glaring eyes. The steel cable was still hanging from its mouth. The riffle popped again for good measure and closed a prolonged chapter of agony.

22

The journey to land was just as drawn out and treacherous as the adventure out to sea. The submerged whaler wallowed and twisted out of control, and the heavy mass in tow made it impossible to accelerate in the rough surf. *Zodiac*, buoyant and not designed for heavy towing, there were times when it behaved like a piece of cork in the strong wind.

Timmy was lying on a low bunk covered with a blanket. He was wrapped up snugly and had overcome his shock. He was unconcerned about the bandage that was lost during the melee but was still guarding his swollen hand like a coveted prize. He settled in a comfortable spot, hugging his wounded leg. No one had disturbed the mat of clotted blood. Bengy stood a little way off, wrapped in a blanket, shoulder deep in his thoughts. He stared at the land growing into view, rising and falling with the motion of the boat that no longer bothered him. He had still not awakened from his most awful experience. The pilot and crew went about their duty deliberately, without questions. After all, there was more than enough evidence to fill in the missing detail.

The VHF transmitter hummed as it was unhitched, and the pilot shifted the dial on the radio.

"Commander! Commander! Voyager, over!"

There was no response, and he repeated his call again.

"Commander! Commander! Voyager, over!"

"Commander here!" came the short reply. "Let's go to working channel…"

A pause.

The pilot shifted the dialed on the radio and responded to the remark.

"Come in, Voyager!"

"I'm approaching the western entrance to the harbor with five persons on board—two passengers, myself, and a crew of two—a partially submerged whaler and a megalodon in tow. Over!"

"A mega—what?"

"A monstrous shark!"

"Roger that! Information noted. Over!"

Everything was seaman's jargon.

The pilot continued the radio conversation.

"One of the passengers is badly injured, so we'll need an ambulance. I repeat, one passenger is badly injured, so we'll need an ambulance. Over!"

"Understood! Ten four! Over and out!"

And the conversation ended.

The weather-beaten crew crept through the breakwater at the entrance of the harbor and inched passed Prince George Dock, where a couple of cruise ships were moored. A few tourists gazed at the boats and concluded that the object astern was a huge log being removed for navigation purposes. They shortened their towline and maneuvered into the basin at the RBDF marine station, where an ambulance and two petrol cars were waiting. A curious crowd stood timidly at a distance, wanting to know what detriment had called up emergency on such a quiet day.

The crowd swelled like water, and soon a multitude was gathered. The word traveled that there was a thing that had stirred a whirlwind of trouble, injured a man, and carried off another kicking and screaming. They wanted to see the culprit and examine its entrails to confirm that someone was indeed devoured, ingested by this creature.

The enormous beast was hitched to a crane and carefully hauled ashore. Its stone-gray eyes sent out a warning from a busted head that seemed like it had been plummeted with a sledgehammer. People winced and gave the ground that was needed. The cable was hanging from its mouth and had dug deep between a cluster of sharp bloody teeth that gave evidence to the unknown atrocious capability of this villain. The stomach was more flaccid than expected, and although there were telltale signs that it had recently mingled in blood, the stomach bulge was not suggestive enough to indicate that it contained a person inside.

The ambulance wailed and left with the rescued men. No other person moved an inch. They wanted to see the contents of the bastard.

A hush came over the crowd as a man was given the awesome task of eviscerating the monster. With gloved hands and a sharp knife, he punctured the soft underbelly and sawed upward through the sandpaper skin. Blood and guts rolled out and slopped his galoshes and a swarm of hungry flies swooped in to feed on the smelly visceral. The butcher brushed them aside and worked expertly. Every face was strained with anxiety, cussing his deliberate effort to make them wait. So far there was nothing significant except the monstrous liver that no one cared about. All eyes were focused on the bulging slimy gray sack that rolled out among the entrails. They waited to see a partly digested human head with gouged-out eyes to confirm the horrid theory associated with this beast, and the butcher played on their imagination. He fiddled around, unwinding the hook attached to the top of the gullet that stitched the mouth of the sack. No one cared about that.

He adjusted his gloves and reset his mask and examined the entrails again for something he knew didn't exist. He fumbled with the repulsive sac and made a small incision at its base. It was like breaking the walls of a tomb. A vomit-like liquid poured out and festered the ground. Hands slapped over mouths and noses, but not one soul turned his head or walked away. The crowd was mesmerized and pressed harder to see the gory contents. With a swipe of the knife, the torture came to an end. It was as if a sewer line had broken. The stench was unbearable. People fanned the air and cupped their mouths and noses and withstood the scent. No one moved. A slight breeze rippled through the leaves of the large silk cotton tree that shaded the area and brought a moment of relief, and the flies buzzed hungrily in competition for the stinking waste. And the crowd stood and waited for the final episode.

The gloved hand dived into the opening of the sac and came out seaweed (long, tawny, and dripping with drool); a gooey license plate; a few mucky scraps of fish head; the short ribs of a small animal, perhaps a cat or a puppy; a black rubber glove; and a tacky sleeve of a woman's dress; the skeletal wrist bones of a hand with a finger bone intact; and the mushy undigested head of a puppy shark.

To satisfy the crowd that everything was removed, the sack was turned inside out. Something dropped with a clink and rolled a few inches and stayed upright in the slime. Everyone stared in silence. The item stood there and beckoned a question. The butcher picked it and rubbed it against his coverall until it was clean. Sparkles of gold glistened through the grime. He held it up and crowed with surprise.

"Well, I'll be damned, if it isn't a ring!" he exclaimed and read the inscription that was barely visible. "Mount Rainer High School SW 1998. It's a graduation ring! It says *high school*." He paused. "Now how the dickens did this get in there?"

The question bounced from person to person. No one had an answer.

They watched in awe as the morbid evidence along with the ring were packed and handed to the police.

"That shark ate someone," a woman called out aloud.

"Damn right, it did!" was the grim response, and the crowd quietly dispersed.

23

$\mathcal{M}$ulling took the clipboard and tried to smile, but he frowned instead. A change came over him as he studied the information. Apprehension clogged his mind, and he hardly knew where to begin, but he had to act quickly.

Calvin was still slumped over in his chair when he felt something abrasive brush against his cheeks. He heard someone calling his name. He wanted to answer, but he couldn't. He wanted to escape, but it felt like his legs were cemented in bucket. The yelping was so close he could feel their breath. One of them leaped for his throat and caught him by the arm. The growl was the most terrible sound he had ever heard. He opened his eyes.

Mullings held him firmly by the shoulders and shook him. He was incoherent and didn't respond immediately. He flinched from the nightmare that was still going on.

"Get up! Get up! Dammit, get up!" Sergeant Mullings was concerned that the prisoner was delirious and had lost a grip on reality. His life, his career, and his future weighed in a balance with this unconscious prisoner. He had to free himself of this responsibility. In the past, he had had people wet their pants, defecated on themselves, and even fainted. But it was only for a short spell, and it was often nothing more than an embarrassment to them. That was the payment for playing tough. Recovery was often quick. He couldn't imagine having a casualty on hand after the recent revelation. The prisoner had to be revived. He had to make amends and discharge him before a sympathetic whistleblower became aware of what had happened.

Mullings unstrapped his prisoner and placed his personal items on the table in readiness for his release.

He shook the listless figure and slapped him delicately on both cheeks. This was ridiculous. The dream persisted. The fat policeman volunteered his help by splashing a couple handful of cold water in the prisoner's face.

Calvin blinked absently and stared at the people in front of him and squealed like a pig. He could not face this torture again.

"No! No! Nooo!" he screamed and squeezed the chair handle and trembled with fear. He didn't realize that they had removed the shackles from his hands and legs.

Mullings was calm and courteous and incredibly pleasant. "Yes, yes, Mr. Meadows," he said. "We believe you. We know you didn't have anything to do with the girl's disappearance. Believe me, we only wanted to see if you knew who was involved." He smiled broadly and lied through his whiskers.

Calvin sniffled and regained his composure. Of all the things he hated, cops were at the top of the list. He wanted nothing to do with them and their deceitfulness. They were the devil, never to be trusted. He eyed them suspiciously and wondered if this was another of their dubious tricks to lure him into complacency, then strike again.

"Get up," Mullings said politely. "You're free to go. Your things are on the table."

Calvin flexed his hands and stretched his feet and realized that he was no longer tied, but he didn't move. Not that he didn't embrace the idea of being free, but it was too ridiculous to believe. A minute ago they were prepared to snip his manpower. He relented. *It's a nasty trick*, he thought and remained seated.

"Go on," urged an encouraging voice. "Dry your feet, put on your shoes, collect your stuff. You're free to go."

He pulled his feet out of the buckets. The water had bleached his feet white, and the temperature had lifted his skin so that every pore was visible. He bent over and fingered his sneakers from under the chair where they sat in a pool of water that was hardly connected to the mopping pail. He fingered his shoes around his heel and felt a burning from a source he couldn't identify. He pulled his trousers uncomfortably over his buttocks and attempted to stand and look angrily at the pool of liquid on the floor under the chair. He had peed on himself. They had forced him to behave like a child who couldn't control wetting his bed. He wanted to pay back.

"Come on, your cab's outside. These officers will help you," Mullings said uneasily. From henceforth, his prisoner was a plague to be avoided. "Hurry, the cab is waiting to take you wherever you want to go…at no charges."

Calvin wanted to refuse. He thought about walking but realized that his feet were too sore to support his weight. Furthermore, in good senses, it was better to accept this rude gesture and escape as far as possible from this hell.

Epilogue

Calvin was unable to prove that he was abused while in police custody as there were no witnesses and no visible injuries to support his claim. For weeks he was unable to comfortably stand; therefore, he could not return to work. During the interim, he lost his job. He later sued the government for $125,000 for wrongful imprisonment and won. The matter was appealed, and the government proposed a settlement of $25,000. Calvin refused the offer and was never remunerated. Today he lives in West Nassau with his wife and child and is doing well in a new career.

The Saladous accepted the tragic death of their daughter and returned to Seattle. They blame no one for the incident but have never since been to Nassau.

About the Author

The author was born in the Commonwealth of the Bahamas where he received his early education and began a career as a teacher. He took an early retirement to venture into private enterprise, which failed miserably. He relocated to Brooklyn, New York, where he lived and worked in several professions including teaching. At the start of the coronavirus pandemic, he transitioned to Florida, where he is currently employed with the Department of Juvenile Justice as a coach/counselor.

Many of his family and friends would be surprised to learn that for most of his childhood and adult life, the author suffered from depression, which was only relieved through writing. His writing was a relief valve and was never designed for publication. This posture however changed when his friend, who later became his wife, accidentally came across one of his stories and was so engrossed that she wanted to read the rest of it. She was as impressed as she was puzzled to find that the rest of the incomplete story was on his computer. She insisted that he publish some of his work. Thus was a start of another career. The author pens his articles from the heart, which has the uncanny ability to touch other hearts.